STORM OF LOVE

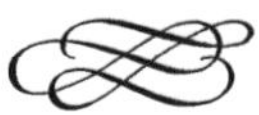

HELEN SUSAN SWIFT

Published 2019 by Liaison – A Next Chapter Imprint

Edited by Terry Hughes

Cover art by Cover Mint

PRELUDE

DUNDEE, SCOTLAND, MAY 1827

Scudding clouds slid over a half-moon, sending shifting shadows across the serried gravestones, while a slight breeze whispered through the near-naked branches of the trees above us.

"This way." Barbara crouched in the shelter of a marble angel, gripping her canvas bag to prevent the contents from rattling. "Keep your head down."

She did not need to warn me. We moved from gravestone to gravestone, keeping in the shadows and cursing the fitful moon. I had hoped for full dark, or at least a cloudy night, but here, nature had not proved our ally as it sent God's lantern to betray our mission.

"This one." Barbara stopped beside a weathered yew. Somewhere in the dark, an owl called, the sound echoing. I pushed away the sinister images that filled my mind.

"Are you certain?" I looked around; it was only a few hours since we had watched the funeral but, in the dark, nothing looked familiar.

"I'm quite certain, Catriona." Crouching at the side of the grave, Barbara opened her bag and handed me a short-handled spade. "Come on, before the grave watchers see us."

Hitching up my skirt, I knelt at the side of the grave and plunged the spade into the earth. "Sorry," I apologised to the man who lay beneath. "I'm dreadfully sorry." The first few spadefuls were easy, and I shovelled the earth to the side, making progress with little effort. At my side, Barbara did likewise, gasping as she delved into the dirt.

I started as the owl called again, the sound eerie in these surroundings.

"Don't stop," Barbara urged. "The watchers could be on patrol at any time."

I glanced up at the squat stone watchhouse, where the flicker of a candle was visible through the small window. Somebody laughed. "I think they're having a celebration in there," I said.

"They bring in whisky against the cold." Barbara shovelled as she spoke. "Now be quiet."

We made rapid progress, creating a hole so deep that soon we had to slide inside. The walls of the grave seemed to close in on me, crumbling slightly, so I shivered at the thought of my own mortality. "We're lucky there's no mortsafe," I said. I had dreaded finding a mortsafe, a heavy cage that relatives placed over the grave to deter such activities as that in which we were engaged.

"Keep quiet! Here." Barbara tapped her spade on something wooden. "We've reached the top of the coffin."

I stopped for a moment as a renewed burst of laughter and snatches of a bacchanalian song came from the watchhouse. Somebody left the building, swinging a lantern. The light bounced from the gravestones, heading in our direction. Peering across the top of the grave, I saw the figure of a tall man in a high hat, striding purposefully with a shotgun in his hand.

"I see you!" He roared. "Get out of that grave!"

"Keep still," Barbara hissed. "For God's own sake, keep still!"

What am I doing here? I asked myself as I crouched on top of the coffin lid with small pieces of earth from the grave crumbling around me. Why am I digging up a grave with a woman I do not like, in the middle of the night? I sighed, and thought back to the beginning of this whole sorry episode and the men who seemed set on ruining my life.

CHAPTER 1

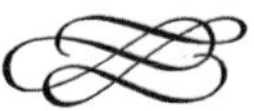

GLACK OF NEWTYLE, SCOTLAND, SPRING 1827

It was raining that morning as I walked southwards towards the Glack of Newtyle, a narrow pass through the Sidlaw Hills in eastern Scotland. I hunched my shoulders, slithered on the muddy track and wished for better weather. As well wish for the moon, of course, in a Scottish spring, but I was so concerned with passing the road and the miles to Dundee that I nearly failed to notice the old man who was walking in front, gathering sticks and adding them to the bundle on his back.

"Halloa," I called to him. "What's to do?"

The poor old fellow nearly jumped out of his skin at the sound of my voice. After he recovered his composure, he turned to face me. "Hello, young lady." His voice was as cracked and ancient as his face, while he peered at me through narrow eyes.

"That's a heavy load you have," I said, thankful for the company, for the Glack can be a lonely place. "Are you going far?"

"As far as I have to," the man answered cryptically. "You're welcome to share my load, young lady."

I balanced half the man's bundle on my shoulder, and we walked side by side for the next mile, with him panting and peching with the weight and me trying to sweeten the journey with a conversation.

"It's a coarse day," I said at last as the old man responded to my sallies with nothing but grunts.

"It's worse than it might be and better than you know," he said at last. "I'll take my sticks now."

I looked around. We had walked perhaps a mile on the deserted road. "Are you sure, Grandfather? There's no house here unless it's in that copse of trees up on the hillside there."

"I said, I'll take my sticks now," the grumpy old fellow repeated and, not wishing to offend him, I obligingly handed them over. He took them with neither a smile nor a thank you, although some trick of the light caught a surprisingly ornate ring on his little finger. "It's a long road behind you."

"It is," I said, looking back instinctively. When I faced forward again, the old man had vanished, presumably into the copse. "Silly old rogue," I said to myself. "Why is he collecting firewood elsewhere when there are scores of trees around him?"

Sighing, I walked on, with the rain now harder than before and the wind buffeting me forward toward distant Dundee.

I stepped aside when I heard the drumbeat of hooves and the grinding of wheels on the road behind me. Fortunately, a nearby tree provided welcome shelter from the rain as I watched the coach whirr past. One can tell the quality of a coach by the noise it makes, from the groaning and creaking of a farmer's cart to the rattle of a decent dog-cart and the whirr of a stagecoach. This coach was different; it purred, even on the rutted road over which it passed. Skilled hands had created that masterpiece of travel, and wealthy people had paid for its construction.

I watched in admiration and not a little envy as this chariot passed me. Drawn by four matching black horses, the coach had two sedate servants sitting in full livery at the back and a tall driver who politely saluted me with a sweeping gesture of his whip. It was a poem on four wheels. I tried to recognise the coat-of-arms, but I was foiled by the spatters of mud that concealed most of the device. I could see only the unusual depiction of an elephant standing on its hind legs. And then I saw the face at the window. He was undoubtedly the most beautiful man I had ever seen, a face that would gracefully adorn any statue of David or even a classical god, an Apollo of the road. I could not help but stare as he looked curiously at me as I stood at the side of the track. Even in that short time, I noticed his bright smile. He raised a slender hand in acknowledgement and then the coach was gone. I watched as it splashed around a bend in the road and vanished beyond a copse of trees.

Sighing, I walked on, wishing that I had been born into a household that could afford such a luxury as a coach. I shook my head, thinking: *Don't be silly, Catriona. Hardly anybody can afford a coach, and you have a good life.* All the same, the image of that splendid carriage with its godlike passenger kept me company for the next mile of the muddy road. The two farm-carts that passed were dull in comparison, even when the collie dog yapped at my heels and looked for attention.

I did not see the woman until I turned a sharp bend. She sat outside her tent, smoking a long-stemmed pipe and looking directly at me.

"Aye, grand weather," she said, lifting the stem of her pipe in acknowledgement.

"It's fine soft rain," I said, wriggling as a drop slithered down my spine to rest uncomfortably at my waist.

"God bless the journey." The woman looked about a hundred, with her wrinkled, weather-battered face and the rags she wore, yet her eyes were as bright as a kitten's as she surveyed me. She replaced her pipe and puffed happily.

"Thank you." I sought an appropriate reply. "God bless the pipe," I said, knowing that it was a feeble response.

The old woman cackled and exhaled blue smoke. "You'll be Catriona Easson, then?"

I started at that. "How do you know my name?"

The woman chuckled again. "I know."

I looked around, where the grey-green slopes of the Sidlaw Hills slid into the rain to my right, and to my left, the ground dipped into a mist-shrouded hollow before climbing toward Kinpurnie Hill. Everything was wet and dismal under the relentless rain.

"Sit beside me, Catriona." The woman tapped the damp ground at her side. "It's all right; I don't bite." Her eyes were intense as she examined me.

Although I wished myself elsewhere, I sat at the woman's side, pulling my legs under me and laying my basket nearby.

"You're going home to Dundee." The woman spoke around the stem of her pipe so that a spurt of smoke accompanied each word.

"Yes," I said. "How do you know that? Who are you?"

"They call me Mother Faa," the woman said. "You've come from Meigle, where you took your mother's baking to your grandmother."

"Yes," I said again. "But how do you know that?"

"I am Mother Faa. How much money do you have with you?"

"A little," I replied cautiously, wondering if half a dozen sorners were hiding in the tent, just waiting to leap out and rob me of all I had. Well, they would be vastly disappointed for I had hardly a penny to scratch myself with, as the saying goes.

"Do you have any silver?"

"I may have." Turning my back so that Mother Faa could not see what I was doing, I opened my pocket-book and scrabbled inside, where a single threepence gleamed silver among the copper pennies and halfpennies.

"Give it here, and I'll tell your fortune," Mother Faa commanded, spreading a hand like a claw. She bit into the threepenny bit and secreted it away somewhere inside her rags. Strangely for one so old and so shabbily dressed, she was clean of person and her clothes had been recently washed.

"I've never had my fortune told before," I wondered what Mr Grieve, the church minister, would think of such a superstitious practice.

"Give me your hand." Mother Faa's claws gripped my wrist and held it tight as she pored over my palm. She turned it this way and that, while a long, if clean, nail traced the various lines.

"What can you see?" Interested despite myself, I found myself relaxing in Mother Faa's company. I could not sense any danger from this woman.

"Everything," Mother Faa said. "I see your past, your present and your future."

"My past is not much to shout about," I said, "my present is wet, and my future is a walk to Dundee."

Mother Faa did not smile at my attempt at humour. "Your past is no secret, Catriona Easson. There is a tragedy there."

"Aye," I said. "My father's ship went down about a year ago. The sea claimed him."

"The sea has a habit of that," Mother Faa said. "The loss of your father affected your mother."

"Yes." I did not say more. My mother's present fragile state of mind was not this woman's business.

"Don't you worry, Catriona. Better times are coming for her and faster than you think."

Mother Faa's words did not convince me. She continued to study my palm. "Your present includes somebody with the letter K." She looked up, her eyes soft. "K?"

"Kenny." I could not hide my smile. "My intended."

"Kenny is your intended." Mother Faa looked into my face. "Yet you are not entirely happy with him."

"I am so," I denied hotly, too hotly.

"You think that he lacks something." Mother Faa ignored my outburst as she pushed my hand away. "You may be right, Catriona. Perhaps he does, but there is another man in your future, and nearly in your present."

"I don't want another man," I said.

"You will," Mother Faa told me with perhaps the hint of a smile. "This man will help you see your Kenny as he truly is."

I shifted, suddenly uncomfortable in the presence of this woman. "I'd better be on my way," I said.

"Wait." Mother Faa seized hold of my sleeve. "You have a lot of good in you, Catriona Easson, and a lot of uncertainty. Be careful in the days ahead for there is a storm coming."

"I'll be careful." I was suddenly desperate to escape from Mother Faa with her gimlet-sharp eyes that saw right through me to find out truths that I hid even from myself. I had no notion what she meant about Kenny. True, he had his faults, but I loved him, didn't I? And was love not blind?

"Choose carefully, Catriona Easson." Mother Faa gave her final unsettling advice. Not until I walked away did I realise that Mother Faa had been wearing the same style of ring on her finger as the old man carrying the sticks. That was curious, if hardly important.

I was not happy as I hurried towards Dundee. Mother Faa's words had disturbed me, so I was less careful where I placed my feet and splashed into more than one of the deep puddles on the road. Sighing, I contemplated the mud that now caked my boots, the bottom of my cape and my skirt. That would take some cleaning when I got home. I was still thinking about the mud on my skirt when I came across the coach for the second time on that eventful journey.

CHAPTER 2

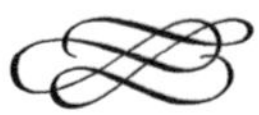

FORFARSHIRE, SCOTLAND, SPRING 1827

The coach stood at an acute angle at the side of the road with the driver and both footmen staring at it and the oh-so-handsome passenger standing beside them, scratching his head and smiling in high good humour.

"Well now," the handsome fellow said, "there's a thing."

Being of a naturally curious nature, I walked across. "What's to do?" I asked.

"Halloa," the handsome fellow greeted me cheerfully. "You don't happen to know anything about chariots, do you?"

"Not a thing," I confessed. "What's happened?"

"We've toppled into the ditch," my handsome traveller said.

"Well, untopple out of the ditch," I advised.

"That's the trouble," the driver said. "We can't."

I stood back, shaking my head. "Surely, with the horses pulling and four strong men pushing, you can get the thing back on the road."

"We can only try."

I could plainly see by their muddy clothes that all the men except my princely passenger had already attempted to push the coach free. Already dirty from the road, I decided to shame him into action, for he looked strong and fit enough to make a difference in such a small matter. "Come along then," I said. "Four strong men and one weak woman may succeed where three strong men have tried and failed."

Wondering if my words could shame the elegant one into action, and without sparing him a glance, I slid behind the coach and applied my slim shoulder, knowing that at least three of the men would follow my example.

"It might be best if you led the horses, miss," the driver said, touching his forehead. "You're only a lightweight."

"Nonsense," I said. "That fellow there," I indicated the handsome one with an imperious wave of my hand, "can lead the horses. He's doing nothing else, after all."

"You're used to giving orders, aren't you," the useless fellow said, but as I had hoped, my words had the desired effect, and he stepped across to the horses, delicately, as if afraid that mud would rot his elegant boots. Men are quite easy to manage if you handle them in the right way.

The driver took charge now. "On my word, lads and, sir, pray, sir, could you could guide the horses to pull in conjunction with us?"

When the handsome one lifted a languid hand in reply, the driver gave a shout, and we all pushed with might and main, whatever that means. In my case, it meant that I laid aside my basket, put my shoulder behind the boot of the chariot and shoved, while the men on either side of me grunted and strained. The coach moved a fraction of an inch, shuddered and sunk back to its original position with the two nearside wheels nearly hub-deep in the mud and the nearside horse floundering up to its hocks.

"We failed," the handsome one said at once.

"So try again," I replied, wondering at the ease with which such a strapping fellow gave up. I did notice him looking at me as if wondering who this strange woman might be.

"On the count of three," the driver shouted. "One, two, three!"

We pushed again, this time to see the wheels slide forward an inch before falling back. The driver swore, softly, and looked to me, ready to apologise for his language.

"I've got an idea," I said. "When the wheels move, somebody can put a stone or something behind them."

"That's your job then," the driver agreed at once. "You're the lightest here, so we'll hold the coach in place while you do so."

I agreed, and one of the footmen cast around for suitable stones, which he placed near to the wheels. All the time, the handsome one patted and soothed the horses while glancing surreptitiously at me from time to time.

The driver nodded to me. "You know what you're doing?"

"I do," I said.

"Right lads," the driver said. "We'll try again. Are you ready, sir?"

The handsome one responded with a smile, and we shoved again. This time, as soon as the wheels shifted, I slid the stone underneath. It was only the width of my thumb, but any gain is better than no gain.

"Now we're getting somewhere," the handsome one said. "Find some more stones." He stood as the footmen scurried around the area, gathering armfuls of rock and getting muddier by the minute. I also watched, with my eyes straying to Adonis, the name I had coined for the useless if god-like figure. Adonis suited him, I thought, being the mortal lover of the goddess Aphrodite. Twice my gaze met his, and we both looked rapidly away.

"Ready, lads and lassie?" The driver was slightly more cheerful as we tried again. This time we lifted the carriage a further fraction so I could slide another stone beneath the wheels.

Inch by inch and with much toil, we moved the coach until, with one final push, it was back on the road and, save for Adonis, we all looked like we had been rolling in mud, which, in a way, we had.

"We've done it," said Adonis, whose boots at least were now less pristine. When he brushed some imaginary dirt from his shoulder with the back of his hand, his gold signet ring boasted a stone as large as the nail of my little finger.

"*We* have," I agreed, emphasising the first word.

Adonis smiled and opened the coach door. "Where are you bound, my pretty one?"

"Dundee," I said, and bit off the words "my handsome man" at the end of my statement.

"That's a coincidence," the handsome one said. "So am I. I'll take you wherever you are going."

At 25 years old, I was not stupid enough to accompany a strange man into a coach without assurances of my safety. "You'll ruin my reputation," I said, shaking my head.

"I will not," my handsome dandy denied. "Come on – you're safe with me. You do know who I am, don't you?"

"I do not." I flinched as a distant peal of thunder indicated that the weather was about to take a turn for the worse. The patter of rain on the roof of the carriage increased.

The dandy tapped the coat-of-arms on the door of his coach. "I am Baird MacGillivray of Mysore House."

"Ah." I knew the name. Mysore House stood on the western fringe of Dundee, off the Perth Road. In common with most folk in the area, I had never seen the house, as it sheltered behind a screen of trees amid a 20-acre garden that included some very exotic plants that the owner had imported from foreign parts.

"My father is Donald MacGillivray, you see." Baird had decided to become garrulous. "He named me after General David Baird."

"I see." I watched as dark clouds gathered above the road to Dundee. The rain had never ceased, but now the drops were heavier, a warning of what was to come. I balanced walking through a torrent against trusting Baird MacGillivray with my reputation, and anything else I hoped to retain until marriage. I touched the long pin I carried in my basket, knowing that I would use it if necessary.

"You will also have a name," Baird said, leaning closer to me, "although I suspect that I already know what it is."

"I am plain Catriona Easson," I said.

Baird gave an exquisite bow. "Well, Catriona Easson, who is

anything but plain, we'll keep the curtains drawn." Baird was very persuasive. "Nobody will know you have accepted an unchaperoned lift from a man, and I promise you faithfully," he swore, pressing a hand over his heart, "that I will act like a perfect gentleman."

When the driver gave me a small nod of encouragement, I could only smile and finger my long pin. "Why then, sir," I said, "I shall gladly accept your offer."

I was only just in time, for the rain-gods opened their vaults and emptied the contents on to poor old Scotland. The rain hammered on to the roof of the coach and bounced off the surface of the road, making the poor horses walk with bowed heads. I pitied the two footmen and the driver on the outside.

"They're used to it." Baird closed the door firmly on my idea of inviting the footmen inside his coach. He tapped the ceiling to signal to the driver, and we pulled away with the wheels sliding this way and that.

"Do you like my little coach?" Baird sat opposite, allowing me to study him properly for the first time. He was indeed handsome, with a firm jawline and a straight nose, yet it was his eyes that held my attention most. They seemed to laugh to me, or perhaps at me, I was not sure which. He was undoubtedly aware of the power they had, for he kept them busy on my face and figure, yet without being in the least offensive.

"Your little coach is magnificent," I said, without any exaggeration. With padded sides in soft dark-red leather and seats of the same material, the carriage interior was as luxurious as anything I had ever seen.

We had to speak loudly to be heard above the sound of the rain. "Thank you," Baird said. "Where are you going?"

"We live in Milne's Close off the Nethergate," I said.

"Oh?" Baird raised his eyebrows. "Have you been there long? No, don't tell me. You said *we*. Is there a Mr Catriona Easson?"

"Not yet," I said. "I was referring to my mother and me." I wondered how much I should tell this Adonis.

"Ah." Baird nodded sagely. "Your mother." I did not know why he emphasised the last word and gave a little smile. "I see. You do not have a husband."

I shook my head. "As I said, Mr MacGillivray, not yet, although I am spoken for."

"That is a great shame," Baird said. "I congratulate you, and congratulate the fortunate man even more so."

I favoured him with a small smile. "He is less fortunate than you believe, Mr MacGillivray, for I have the very devil of a temper."

Baird leaned back in his seat to survey me before he replied. "I wager that your temper would be worth watching, Miss Easson."

"I wager it would be worth avoiding, Mr MacGillivray," I returned, somewhat tartly, with my hand firmly closed on the pin in my basket.

"Touché," Baird said with his eyes more intense than I had expected.

We lurched to the side as the coach slithered. Baird laughed as he righted himself. "Are you all right?"

"It's impossible to get hurt in here," I said. "The coach is so well padded."

Baird laughed again. He seemed to find everything amusing. "I like to travel in comfort. It's one of the benefits of wealth."

I raised my eyebrows, not used to people boasting of their financial situation. Although it was somewhat vulgar, it was also refreshingly honest. I could not help my smile. "It's better to be comfortable than the reverse," I indicated the battering rain outside. "I wager that your footmen had rather be inside than out."

"I do not doubt that," Baird replied at once, "but four would be rather a crowd, don't ye know, and I rather like having you all to myself."

"I'm nothing special," I said.

Baird smiled and changed the subject. "We can't take you home looking like that," he said. "Your mother will be most displeased to see her daughter in such a state." He smiled. "Why, she'll think you and I have been rolling in the mud together."

I looked down at myself. The mud had dried on my cloak and skirt, leaving me looking like a wandering tinker rather than a respectable churchgoer. I contemplated what Baird had said and wondered if he was Mother Faa's man in my future and nearly in my present. "I'll have to brush myself down the moment I get home."

"I can do better than that," Baird said. "Come to Mysore House and we'll get you properly cleaned up."

"I can't do that." The thought of stepping inside a strange man's house was appalling to me.

"You're safe with me," Baird repeated his earlier assurance. His smile returned. "If the chariot impressed you, I am sure you'll love Mysore House."

Turning away, I looked out of the window with my mind in a whirl. I had long wanted to see what Mysore House was like, and now I was being offered to step inside, although it would probably be only the servant's quarters. If Baird had wished to take advantage of me, he had shown no sign during the past half-hour in the coach. Indeed, he kept a respectable distance away and even when the jolt had pushed us together, he had extricated himself in seconds. On the other hand, Mother would be fascinated by any snippet I could tell her about Mysore House and, of course, I was never backward in coming forward to satisfy my curiosity.

"Thank you, Mr MacGillivray," I said. "I should be glad to accept your very kind offer."

"Then that is settled, Miss Easson." As Baird sat back in his seat with a face like a cat who found himself in a whole dairy of cream, I wondered if I had made the correct decision.

Although I must have walked along the Perth Road a hundred times, it was utterly different travelling in a coach, with most other traffic making way for us. Truly, wealth did give a feeling of power. I wondered what it would be like enjoying such luxury as a right, and I rather enjoyed leaning back in the yielding cushions and staring out of the window as the rain eased.

The driver steered us around to the lodge that guarded the tall iron gates of Mysore House. I had often stood on the outside and watched, but now the lodge-keeper opened the gates for us and then we were rolling up the curved drive with the iron-shod wheels grating over gravel and the grounds spreading like a botanical heaven.

At a signal from Baird, we stopped opposite Mysore House. Baird threw open the coach door, so I had a better view of his home. "Well," he said with justifiable pride in his voice, "what do you think of Mysore?"

"It's wonderful," I said. "I've never seen anything like it."

The name, Mysore, should have given me a clue that this house would be different from every other house in knew. While the centre of Dundee was composed of grey, weathered tenements and narrow closes of two-storey houses, the suburbs had their quota of substantial Georgian or Regency square-fronted mansions. Mysore House was unlike any of them. It was how I would imagine an Indian palace to appear if it had been plucked from that exotic, feverish land and transported bodily to our damp climate. It was a place of unusual towers and strangely elaborate balconies, of fancy ironwork and pointed doors. The coat of arms above the main entrance was carved in granite and freshly painted, with two elephants standing over a shield on which sat a cat with its right paw over its tail.

"It's nothing like anywhere I've ever seen," I said.

I heard the delight in Baird's chuckle.

"I thought you'd like it," he said.

I pointed to the coat of arms. "Why the cat?" I asked. "I can understand the elephants from your Indian experiences, but what is the reason for the cat?"

"We are associated with the Clan Chattan confederation," Baird explained. "That means the clan of the cat."

I nodded. "It's very distinctive."

Baird grinned. "Come on. We'll get you cleaned up, and I'll give you the grand tour."

I looked at him in astonishment. The best I had expected was the loan of a brush in the servants' quarters. "Do you mean it?"

"I most certainly do," this strange Adonis said. "Come on, Miss, eh, Easson. We'll leave the servants to care for the coach and horses."

The smiling, insipid fop of the road had gone, with an energetic man taking his place as Baird strode up the seven steps to the main door of Mysore House. As if by magic, a faceless servant opened the door.

"Thank you, Henry," Baird said.

I remained outside, clutching my near-empty basket, feeling slightly hesitant until Baird gestured me forward.

"Come in and welcome, Miss Easson." He raised his voice to a shout. "Mrs Mahoney!"

Rather than pay attention to the antics of Baird, I slid through the pointed door and stared around me at the interior of Mysore House. The entrance hall was vast, with great pillars soaring to an ornately plastered ceiling, while twin marble staircases provided access to the upper floors. Pointed arches topped all the doors, but it was the details that drew my attention. The architect had set niches into the panelled walls, and a statue stood in every niche. Some were only a foot tall, while the largest was a man-sized multi-armed figure that could only have been some exotic Indian god. On closer inspection, I saw that it was a goddess, while others of the statues were of male or female figures that left very little to the imagination.

"Good, aren't they?" I had not realised that Baird was watching me with a broad smile across his face. "Father and Mother brought them back from India with them."

I stepped back from a particularly detailed sculpture of a very masculine man. "They are very... I've never seen anything like them before." I could feel the blood rushing to my face. Did respectable people have such objects in their houses?

"That one is mother's favourite," Baird lifted the male statue.

I could feel my face burning as I wondered what to say. "They're different from the usual classical statues from Greece and Rome," I said at last.

"Here's Mrs Mahoney now," Baird murmured as he replaced the statue.

"What is it?" Mrs Mahoney was between 40 and 50, tall, slender and handsome with a complexion that suggested she spent much of her time out of doors. She looked at me, and then at Baird. "Good heavens, Mr Baird! Who is this you have dragged in?"

"This, Mrs Mahoney," Baird gestured to me as if I were some prize specimen of horseflesh or his latest artistic creation, "is Miss Catriona Easson of Nethergate. Without her magnificent and generous help, we would never have got home today. Indeed, we would have been floundering in the mud, murdered by gypsies or struck by lightning."

"Oh, I dare say," Mrs Mahoney surveyed me through narrow blue eyes.

"If Miss Easson had not helped us," Baird elaborated, "she would not be in such a mess, so I believe it is our responsibility to clean her up."

When Mrs Mahoney frowned, Baird took her aside and spoke in tones too low for me to hear. Mrs Mahoney started, looked over to me and nodded. "I'll take care of it," she said. When she turned back to me, her attitude had completely altered.

"Mr Baird informed me that you would be more comfortable meeting his mother if you were less muddy," she said, now smiling. "Please come this way, Miss Easson." Mrs Mahoney turned on her heel and was half a dozen strides away from me before I could even gather my wits.

I hurried to catch up, nearly slipping on the glass-smooth marble floor. "I am not staying to see Mrs MacGillivray," I protested to Mrs Mahoney's fast-retreating back.

"Go on," Baird whispered. "You'll be glad that you did."

Sighing, and wishing I had chanced the rain rather than accept a lift in the coach, I hurried to catch up with her, nearly slipping on the glass-smooth marble floor. We descended a single flight of stairs to a long stone-flagged room where a pump provided water for a sink and a long trestle table boasted half a dozen brushes of various sizes. A bright fire in the corner kept the spring chill at bay.

"Right then, Miss Easson." Mrs Mahoney was all brusqueness. 'We'll soon have you clean, if hardly presentable, for the master and mistress."

"I have no intention of meeting Mr and Mrs MacGillivray," I said, tartly. "I came here only on Baird's insistence."

"What you've been doing is no business of mine," Mrs Mahoney said. "I won't ask any questions, and you won't need to tell me any lies."

"I don't tell lies,' I said, slightly irritable. I could feel my temper rising.

Mrs Mahoney's cynical grunt told me what she thought of that statement. "Strip off your clothes, Miss Easson, and while you're washing your person, I'll have your clothes brushed, washed, dried and pressed."

"You can't do that," I protested.

"Oh, I won't be doing it," Mrs Mahoney told me. "The maids will do the work. I shall ensure they do it properly."

"I was not going to stay," I said. "My mother is waiting for me."

"Mr Baird has already sent word to your *mother* that you are here," Mrs Mahoney said. "Now off with your clothes, or I'll have the maids take them off for you."

I heard a giggle behind me and saw half a dozen maidservants, aged from 14 to 30, waiting for me.

"Come along, Miss," the oldest encouraged. "The quicker you start, the quicker we'll have you ready."

Wondering how on earth I had got myself into this predicament, I began to strip off, with the maids clustering around offering advice and help. They whisked away every scrap of clothing the instant I removed it and immediately began work. I expected titters of laughter as I stood as nature intended, but five of the maids were too busy washing my clothes while the oldest brought me a deep basin of warm water, soap and a selection of cloths and sponges.

"Stay close to the fire," she urged me. "Would you like me to help you?"

"I can manage," I replied. I washed and dried quickly, strangely relaxed amid so much female company, with Mrs Mahoney standing sentinel, giving an occasional sharp order that had the servants scurrying to obey. I also noticed that she ran her gaze up and down the length of my body. Well, she could do that from Monday to Christmas for all I cared; I had nothing to be ashamed of in that department. If anything, I was slightly too ample in certain places.

"You have fine child-bearing hips," was Mrs Mahoney's somewhat bizarre remark.

"It runs in the family," I replied, trying not to feel embarrassed.

Mrs Mahoney's nod could have signified approval.

By the time I had got myself washed, the maids began returning my clothes to me in a steady stream, with the most delicate already dried by the fire and pressed, and the others nearly so. I had never seen such efficiency, and said so, once I was decently covered.

Mrs Mahoney gave a bleak smile. "Many things are different in Mysore House, as you will find out."

"I really ought to leave," I said as I accepted my travelling cloak from a smiling maid. It looked better than new.

"As I have told you, we've sent word to your mother, so you've no reason to fret," Mrs Mahoney said. "There is a place set for you at the table." She nearly smiled again. "I know that you would not wish the servants to waste all that effort, especially when Mr and Mrs MacGillivray would dearly like to meet the woman who helped their son."

I stood for a moment as the servants tidied away all the washing equipment and hurried off to whatever duties next awaited them. Although my mother had not been herself since the sea took father, I was sure she would be all right for a few hours and, to be honest, I had long wished to see the inside of Mysore House. Anyway, I was intrigued at the prospect of meeting Baird's parents.

"Thank you," I said. "I'd be delighted to come along if you are sure the family will not object to my uninvited company." I could feel my heart thumping at the thought of attending a meal in such a grand house, for the classes do not mix well. Each should stay with its own.

In the event, the meal was stranger than any I had been to before, or since. Where I had expected formality, Wedgewood bone china and stiff faces, instead I found a long table within a room more delightful than any I had even imagined before, with light décor around me and a crystal chandelier swinging slowly above. As a servant ushered me inside, I heard strange music emanating from behind a screen in the corner. A bevy of servants curtseyed or bowed as I entered.

"You look better without the mud." Wearing the most elegant of clothes, Baird stepped forward to greet me, smiling and with a hand outstretched. He looked me up and down for a moment. "Do you like our music? It's Indian. Father and mother brought back a love for Indian music from the East. It's rather unusual to the ear at first, but grows on you until you prefer it to anything else." He gave his characteristic grin. "I've known little else since childhood, so it's normal for me."

I smiled back, still thinking about Mother and very much ill at ease in these unusual surroundings, but determined to absorb all that I could. I knew I would never be back inside this building.

With that Oriental music filling my head and Baird smiling to me across the width of the table, I waited for the arrival of Mr and Mrs MacGillivray. Although their coach was sometimes seen travelling around Dundee, the MacGillivrays were strangers in the city; indeed, nobody had ever seen Mrs MacGillivray. I recalled some of the rumours that claimed the lady of the house was Indian, or that Mr MacGillivray had a bevy of Asian wives rather than only one, so I waited in some apprehension for Baird's parents to appear. The music rose to a crescendo, with much strumming of strings and blowing of horns and then the pointed door opened.

Mrs Mahoney stepped in, completely spoiling the drama of the moment.

"Good evening, Baird." She had changed into a long silken dress that enhanced her height and, if anything, increased her dignity.

With a significant glance at me, Baird nodded. "Good evening, Mother." Perhaps it was the emphasis he put on the final word that rammed the message home. Mother?

"Good evening, Miss Easson."

"Good evening," I replied automatically, wondering what was happening.

Mrs Mahoney's smile was a mirror image of Baird's. "Yes, Miss Easson, I am Mrs MacGillivray. I do apologise for the deception, but I wished to see what you were like behind your manners."

I felt myself colouring and replied tartly: "Well, you certainly saw more of me than most." I mentally cringed at the memory of standing naked beside Baird's mother.

Mrs Mahoney's smile broadened. "You have no reason to be ashamed."

I tried to keep my temper under control, although I was tempted to turn around and walk out.

"My husband will arrive shortly." Mrs Mahoney was still assessing me when the door opened again. I was not sure what to expect – perhaps a man in the dress of an Indian rajah. But Mr MacGillivray was as ordinary a man as one could ever hope to meet on the streets of Dundee. He was of medium height and build and his only distinguishing features were the deep tan of his face and the intelligence of his brown eyes that looked exactly the same as Baird's.

"And here is Barbara," Mrs MacGillivray said as a young woman joined us. "Now, we are ready to begin."

Barbara would have turned men's heads in any house in the land. A tall, statuesque, auburn-haired beauty, she walked into the dining room like a queen approaching her throne and took her place at the table. Her glance at me was a combination of contempt and curiosity as if I was something the cat refused to drag in.

"This is my daughter, Barbara." Mrs MacGillivray could not disguise the pride in her voice.

I gave a perfunctory curtsey.

"Have you met Catriona Easson?" Mrs MacGillivray asked.

I was sure that Barbara gave a little start before she replied. "No." We looked at each other with instant and mutual dislike.

"Miss Easson helped when our chariot got stuck in a ditch," Baird said cheerfully.

"Oh, how interesting," Barbara commented blandly, although she did not look interested in the slightest. We did not speak to each other again.

The meal was as ordinary as Mr MacGillivray, a procession of soup, fish and sweet, with claret and other French wines as the musicians played in the background and we exchanged polite conversation.

"Do you have many horses?" Mr MacGillivray asked me.

"Not even one," I replied. "Even when father was alive, money was tight."

"Of course. How did your father die?" Baird looked directly at me.

"The sea took him," I said.

"I believe I read about that," Mrs MacGillivray said.

"I didn't know his name was in the papers." That surprised me. Father had been the mate of a coasting brig, sailing from Dundee to London and all points in between. Newspapers do not often print the names of hardworking and honest men.

I saw Baird and Mrs MacGillivray exchange glances.

"It was a terrible thing," Mrs MacGillivray said.

"Any life cut short is a tragedy," I agreed.

"You can shelter in Mysore House as long as you wish," Mrs MacGillivray said. "Baird was quite right to bring you here."

"Thank you," I said, "I'm sure I will be fine." Although I was not sure why these MacGillivrays were so attentive to my needs, or why I should desire to shelter in Mysore House, I began to like them, despite, or perhaps because of their peculiarities. For the remainder of that meal, I spoke when required, felt Mrs MacGillivray's gaze on me as if I was being examined or tested, and watched the grandfather clock in the corner slowly tick away the evening.

"You appear bemused," Mr MacGillivray made a rare contribution to the conversation in his pleasant, well-modulated voice. "What were you expecting?" He smiled. "I am aware of the rumours surrounding Mysore House, and its occupants."

"I was not sure," I answered truthfully.

"Did you expect dusky servants in flowing saris, a tiger wandering the grounds and a master wearing a huge turban with a diamond in the centre?" Mr MacGillivray was gently mocking.

"Perhaps something of the kind," I admitted.

Baird was first to laugh. "My father is a nabob, not a rajah. He made money in India; he did not become an Indian."

"Do you not wish to go to India?" I tried to find out more about Baird. "I have heard that people can live like kings there."

"They can," Baird said. "And they can also die of a hundred different diseases." He shook his head. "No. At present I hope to extend our trading here in Dundee." Baird surprised me with his decisive reply. "I know we are further north than most ports that trade with the East, but I am sure there is a market for Indian raw materials in Scotland, or for our manufactured products in India."

I felt my hosts' attention focus on me and scraped my mind for words. "Would you not be better moving into an established trade? Dundee has a long-standing linen trade with the Baltic, or you could sail to Norway for timber, Spain for fruit or France for wine."

I felt Mr MacGillivray's attention quicken. "Do you take an interest in such matters?" He asked. "That is unusual for a young woman. I know that most ladies prefer accomplishments such as sewing or painting."

"I find the world an interesting place," I replied. "And sewing and painting can be such dull occupations."

"How refreshing," Mrs MacGillivray gave Baird a meaningful look. "I do approve of this young woman, Baird."

Baird grinned as if he had personally trained me in my list of accomplishments.

"It's hardly a woman's place to have such interests," Barbara spoke to the chandelier above rather than to me. "It veers toward the masculine, I would think."

"Better than being empty-headed and vacuous," I replied with the most charming smile I could muster.

"I am glad to be neither of such things," Barbara replied with her eyes dark with dislike. "Do you have any feminine interests?"

"I am interested in many things," I replied, keeping my temper under control, "including minding my own business."

As Barbara opened her mouth to retaliate, Mrs MacGillivray intervened. "My daughter likes to make jewellery." I heard the pride in Mrs MacGillivray's voice. "And she supervises the maids in making dresses."

Ready to extend an olive branch, I nodded across the table to Barbara, although secretly I was not impressed by her supposed accomplishments. She returned my nod with a cold stare, and we returned to the serious business of eating, with Baird seeming to inspect every mouthful I swallowed. At last, the meal ended, and before the inevitable drinking began, I reminded the MacGillivrays that my mother was waiting for me.

"The chariot will take you home," Mr MacGillivray's smile was more restrained than that of his son. "After all, we have to take care of Baird's young lady."

The words awoke what had only been suspicion. I glanced at Baird, hoping that he would provide clarification, but he only smiled all the wider. "I am afraid there has been a misunderstanding," I said. "Baird and I met by chance only today.'

"Oh, we know that Miss, eh, Easson," Mr MacGillivray said.

"The first meeting is always the most important. Why, I remember the first time I chanced upon Mrs MacGillivray, or Miss Mahoney as she was then."

"Not now, MacGillivray." Mrs MacGillivray spoke with some severity. "This is neither the time nor the place."

"Maybe later." Mr MacGillivray spoke directly to me. "When Mrs MacGillivray is not here." I was pleased that Mrs MacGillivray joined in the laughter. Only Barbara did not seem amused.

"If love does not spark at first, it might never." Mrs MacGillivray was still smiling. "Now, you're fretting to be away. Don't be a stranger, Miss Easson. There is always a welcome here for you."

"I have never been so kindly received," I said. "I wish there were a way I could return your generosity."

"There is no need." Mrs MacGillivray touched my arm. "All I ask is that you look fondly on our Baird."

"I have the warmest regard for Mr Baird MacGillivray," I said.

"Well then," Mrs MacGillivray said. "I have hopes that your regard may blossom into love."

"I am sorry," I said. "I am already betrothed."

"That's all right," Baird said easily. "I'll persuade you to alter your affections. I've taken a great affection for you, Miss Easson, and I mean to have you as my wife."

CHAPTER 3

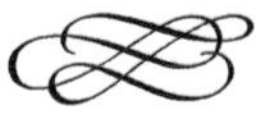

NETHERGATE, DUNDEE, AUTUMN 1827

I lay in bed that night with images from the previous days flashing through my brain. I heard Baird's words again and again: "I mean to have you as my wife."

Well, my brave Adonis, I thought, *I am already spoken for and have no intention of altering my affections for Baird MacGillivray or anybody else.* However, coupled with Mother Faa's warnings about Kenny, I was more than a little concerned.

The events passed through my mind in a constant procession, repeating endlessly, as I tossed and turned in my narrow bed. I saw again the old man carrying his sticks, Mother Faa with her wise, wrinkled face, Baird MacGillivray and his parents and the luxury of Mysore House.

"I can't make sense of it," I said as my mother came in to see what was troubling me.

"You can't make sense of what?" she asked, and I poured out the entire story, not sparing her any details. Mother listened without interruption, nodding at all the right places, although she had been far from well ever since Father died.

"So he wants you for a wife, does he?" The last year had aged

Mother so that she looked worn compared to Mrs MacGillivray, although they must have been of similar ages.

"That's what he said, Mother."

Mother pursed her lips. "I'll wager Kenneth Fairweather will have something to say about that!"

I said nothing. I would love my Kenny to go riding to Mysore House like a knight on a white charger, slapping Baird with his gauntlet to challenge him to a duel. However, I knew that would not happen. Kenny was not that sort of man and besides, I had rather liked Baird, for all his faults. I pondered for a moment. What sort of man was Kenny? Had Mother Faa been correct; was I not entirely happy with my betrothed? Did I think he lacked something?

"Choose carefully," Mother Faa had said, and: "This man will help you see your Kenny as he truly is."

If Baird was the mysterious "man" how would he enable me to see Kenny as he truly was? I did not know, and when I asked my mother, she sighed and sat beside my bed.

"All right, Catriona," Mother said. "This Baird MacGillivray fellow might be all hot air and bombast. Forget him and concentrate on what you know. Kenneth Fairweather is a good man, and the chances are you will never see Baird again. After all," she continued, glancing around the tiny room, "it's not as if he's in our social circle."

That was true. We had moved out of our four-roomed house and into this much smaller place in Milne's Close when Father's death decreased our income by two-thirds. Milne's Close was no worse and no better than the places in which most people in Dundee lived, although far different from Mysore House or the mansions along Perth Road and Broughty Ferry. It was unlikely Baird had ever been in Milne's Close, and even less likely that he would ever visit in future. With that reassuring thought, I turned on my side.

I could forget that handsome gentleman with his coach and fancy house. It had been a pleasant interlude in my life, a look at a different way of life and nothing more. Tomorrow I could return to the humdrum reality of life as a mill hand in Dundee and hope that someday Kenny and I could tie the knot, or get spliced, as Kenny called it.

I sighed. Mysore House was a dream. I could never aspire to such luxury and would never fit in with such people. A single visit was one thing, permanent residence was quite different. Baird MacGillivray would have to live with the disappointment of finding somebody else to share his life, and I would settle for dull, monosyllabic Kenneth Fairweather.

Settle for him? I loved the man. Didn't I?

Of course, I loved him; I had known him since childhood. I must love him. Mother Faa was wrong.

The sound of my mother crying woke me later that morning, and I lay awake. It was not an uncommon sound. She had cried most nights over the past 12 months, and she always slept fitfully and woke with a forced smile to face the next day. I rose to make up the fire and put the kettle on; a cup of tea was the only salve I knew to settle mother's nerves.

As the kettle bubbled on the fire, I glanced at the newspaper that lay on the table. Advertisements filled the front page, as always, so I flicked to the inside pages to find something of interest. There were the usual snippets to entice the casual reader: the mail coach between Stirling and Edinburgh had overturned, Lady Catherine Eastwick had disappeared on the day her father died, there had been a spate of mysterious murders in Edinburgh's Old Town and the ice in the Baltic had finally melted. This last piece interested me, for it affected Kenny, so I read further. The melting ice meant that the Baltic ports were open for trade and the ships from the Scottish east-coast ports could sail in for flax or timber. That meant Kenny's vessel would be off soon; I started as the kettle boiled over, spilling water into the fire with a great hiss. Using a cloth to protect my hand, I lifted the kettle from the fire and poured the water on to the tea-leaves in the pot.

I always woke Mother with a cup of strong tea to help her cope with the day. As I rose from the table, I decided to change the tablecloth and found out that mother had another reason for grief apart from her widowhood. We always kept the house spotless, however poor we were, for mother insisted that we were respectable people, whatever our circumstances. When I removed the old tablecloth, I found an official-looking letter hidden underneath, with the seal already broken. Knowing that Mother was now asleep in the box-bed she had once shared with father, I opened the letter and read it by the flickering flame of a candle.

Notice of Eviction.
It has been noted that you are now three weeks behind with your rent. Unless the balance is paid in full by the end of this week, you will be evicted from the house you presently occupy.
The balance due is 15 shillings.
William Graham, Factor, for James Milne, landlord.

I took a deep breath. I knew we were struggling for money but had no idea that things had become so bad.

Fifteen shillings; that was two weeks' wages for me; three weeks' wages for mother. I counted the money in my purse; ninepence. I doubted that Mother had more. Where could we possibly raise 15 shillings by the end of the week?

The answer was obvious. We could not. For one instant, I thought about the luxury of Mysore House; the MacGillivrays would not notice 15 shillings. They probably spent that in wine or food in a couple of days. But we lived in reality, and somehow we had to find 15 shillings.

I forced a bright smile as I woke Mother, and knew her answering smile was equally false. Neither of us wished to upset the other, and I left for work with a heavy weight pressing on my heart. The excitement of the previous day was only a memory.

If there is anything more depressing than standing on a murky quayside before dawn, waiting to say goodbye to the man you intend to marry, then I don't know what it is. In my experience, it always rains when Kenny's brig puts out to sea as if God himself was weeping for my sorrow. I stood on the greasy stone slabs with the rainwater dripping from the rim of my hood and pattering off the shoulders of my green travelling cape as Kenny made the final preparations to leave Dundee for the Baltic.

I watched Kenny's confident movements as he climbed from the deck to the main topsail, showing a young seaman how to make sure the sail was furled correctly. With complete confidence, he moved along the yardarm to check something else before returning to the mast and swarming down the ratlines to leap back to the deck. All the time I watched, the vessel creaked and ropes slapped in the wind that rattled the heavy wooden blocks and whined through the rigging.

"Aye," a bearded old man said to me. "She's a lively one."

"Aye, she is that," I agreed without having the slightest idea what the old fellow meant. I seem to attract old men, who slouch up to me and speak without even the barest of introductions.

"She'll be worse before she's better," the old man nodded at his own sagacity.

"I don't doubt it," I agreed, wishing my bearded companion would wander off and bother somebody else.

"But old *Admiral Duncan* will weather her." When the old man pointed the stem of his pipe towards Kenny's brig, I realised that he had been talking about the boisterous weather and telling me that *Admiral Duncan* would get through unscathed.

"Yes, I think so," I said, warming slightly to the man. "Do you know the ship?"

"Old *Duncy*'s a brig, miss, not a ship." The old man replaced the pipe in his mouth. "A ship has three masts and a brig only two." He launched into technical details about rigging that frankly left me cold. I only wanted to see Kenny for a few moments before he sailed and did not care how many masts, sails and spars his vessel had or did not have.

"You'll be young Fairweather's lady," the old man eventually said.

"Yes," I agreed. "I am Kenny Fairweather's betrothed."

"Aye." The man put a great deal of expression into that one word, as many Scotsmen can do. In the right mouth, the word "aye" can mean anything from a simple yes to great disapproval, sarcasm, a threat or high praise. This old man sounded as if he mingled all the meanings at one time. "He's a soundish man, is young Fairweather."

"Do you know him well?" My interest grew at anything to do with Kenny, especially praise.

"Aye. I'm Tam MacNaughton."

"Are you indeed?" I expressed surprise, although the name meant nothing at all to me.

"You'll ken my name." Tam MacNaughton spoke with perfect assurance. "I kent auld Fairweather, that's young Fairweather's faither."

"Ah," I said. "You knew Kenny's father." I wished Kenny would finish whatever nautical task he was performing and come ashore to rescue me from this garrulous old goat.

"That's what I said. And no man's as good as his faither, Never was, never will be." Tam MacNaughton gave a nod as if that settled the matter. "Young Fairweather is the same. He's a steady enough man, but that's all." MacNaughton looked me up and down, shaking his head. "Aye, you're about right for him, like for like and if you're no great benefit to the world, you're no great sorrow, either." He slouched away to spread his good cheer elsewhere.

Well, thank you for the encouragement, Tam MacNaughton, I thought. *I'm no great benefit to the world and Kenny's only a steady enough man.*

It was a relief when Kenny stepped ashore from *Admiral Duncan.* Dressed in his seafaring garb of loose white trousers and a stained canvas jacket, he looked little different from any other member of the crew, except he was a little taller.

"Catriona," he spread his tarry arms, unsmiling.

"Kenny." I submitted to his embrace, knowing I would have to scrub hard to remove the tar-stains later. Honestly! The things I had to do for love. "When are you sailing?"

"On the next tide." Kenny released me and glanced up at the sky. "Weather's moderating. There'll be an offshore breeze to ease us out of the Tay."

I knew enough about sailoring to understand that. The wind would come from the land, so pushing *Admiral Duncan* out to sea. Coupled with an ebbing tide, that meant Kenny would be able to get away faster. That was good for his voyage, although less cheerful for me.

"Entering and leaving the Tay is always tricky." Kenny continued his oh-so-romantic conversation. "Captain Jackman's negotiated a fee for a pilot to take us beyond the Abertay Sands and Buddon Ness."

"I'll miss you," I said, hoping my declaration might be reciprocated.

"We should only be a few weeks," Kenny said, as if that made things any better. "A quick trip across the North Sea, through the Skagerrak and the Kattegat, across the Baltic, pick up a cargo of flax and home."

The names meant little to me, although I recognised them as channels around Denmark. In common with most people in Dundee, I had grown up with the docks as central to the town. While other towns had pigeons, Dundee had seagulls, and while Edinburgh had its castle and Glasgow its river, Dundee had the docks and the Firth of Tay, that is, what English folk would call the estuary of the River Tay. Even our Town House faced two ways, with one door opening to the High Street and the other looking out over the sea.

"When is high tide?" I asked.

"In about an hour," Kenny glanced over his shoulder at his first love, his ship. I was aware that in any contest, I could not compete with *Admiral Duncan.* I knew better than even to try. If any of the Fairweather family were cut, they would bleed saltwater and tar.

"Do you like *Admiral Nelson*?" Kenny nodded towards a much

larger, three-masted vessel that lay in the dock. "She's the latest of the company's vessels, brand new, built in Dundee and intended to be the fastest and best ship in the company's fleet."

I made the appropriate noises of admiration. *Admiral Nelson* was about half again the size of Admiral Duncan, with her three masts towering above most in the dock. In common with most British ships, she was black with a white trim.

"Tam Galbraith's her master," Kenny said. "He's a good man."

Kenny was not a man for small talk. Honestly, I sometimes wondered what I ever saw in him. He was no conversationalist and about as romantic as a barrel of tar.

"She looks a fine vessel," I said, wishing I could get Kenny to talk about something other than the sea.

"I'd love to sail in her," Kenny said with enthusiasm.

"Maybe you will, next voyage."

"Maybe." Kenny sounded doubtful. "Uncle Jim would have liked to see her." Kenny's expression altered at the mention of his uncle, who lay dying in his bed even as we spoke.

"He might pull through," I said. "Your Uncle Jim is a fighter."

"Nobody can fight what he's got," Kenny said. "I doubt I'll see him again. He's a good man." For a moment, I saw the decency behind Kenny's tough sea-exterior, the real man with whom I had fallen in love years ago, but who rarely showed through. "Uncle Jim was my first master, a shellback of the first order, and he taught me all I know. I'd like to be there when he goes."

"He knows you love him," I said.

Kenny rewarded me with a withering look. Mates of Baltic traders did not weaken themselves with such thoughts. They loved only their ships, with the occasional, the very occasional, splinter of emotion saved for their women. Perhaps Mother Faa had been right; I was not entirely happy with this man who lacked passion for me. I compared him mentally with Baird, hated myself and quickly pushed the thought away.

"You'd better get back to work, Kenny." It hurt to say these words;

it hurt to step back from Kenny with his open, clean-shaved face with the clear grey eyes. I forced a smile. "Your brig needs you."

"She does." Kenny looked glad to return to his work.

"I watched him leap on to *Admiral Duncan*, shouting orders to the crew as he checked the rigging and peered into the holds. The dock was busy, as always, with Baltic brigs, great three-masted south-Spainers ready to sail halfway around the world, grimy colliers and weather-beaten coasters, open rafts that carried stone from the Kingoodie Quarry to rebuild the city, an ice-scarred whaling ship and the ubiquitous fishing craft.

I heard Kenny's voice giving commands as a grimy steam tug puffed up and attached a tow to *Admiral Duncan*. Captain Jackman, tall and imperious, stood beside the helmsman, giving orders that Kenny translated to the crew. When *Admiral Duncan* cast off, I watched her nose away from the quay, with an officious-looking pilot at the wheel and a tug towing her.

That's my man going away again, I thought. *That's Kenny, and he hardly had a word to spare for me.*

I watched the tug manoeuvre *Admiral Duncan* into the roads, where the lively breeze threw spindrift across the sandbanks that made the entrance to the Firth so dangerous. Kenny turned then, and I waved from my stance at the pier head, allowing my white handkerchief to flutter farewell. For one second, I thought he saw me. He raised a hand and then returned to his work, and my heart felt as if it would break. By that one gesture, that single second he could spare, Kenny had reaffirmed his commitment to me. Bittersweet emotions surged through me; the pleasure of being acknowledged and the aching sense of loss I always experienced when Kenny sailed away.

I stood there until *Admiral Duncan* eased into the Firth with the spray breaking from her and the boisterous wind throwing grey-green seas against her hull, and I stood there until she vanished from sight. After that, I stood there still, holding my futile handkerchief in the air. I wished desperately for some turn of fortune that would see my

Kenny return quicker so we could be together for longer than a few stolen minutes. I hoped for some reciprocal show of affection from the stony-faced man to whom I had pledged my love. I wished that he would even give me some token of his love, such as a ring or a brooch. I wished... I did not know for what I wished, except that I wished the world to change for the better, and I did not know how to make that happen.

At last, when I was frozen to the bone by wind and rain, I moved away, with the rain disguising the tears on my cheeks and my legs stiff from standing still.

CHAPTER 4

DUNDEE DOCKS, SPRING 1827

The carriage was outside the dock gates, with the early morning sun reflecting from the newly washed body and the matched horses stamping in their traces. I did not need the distinctive coat-of-arms on the door to tell me the owner.

"Miss Easson." Baird sat in the doorway, puffing on a long cheroot. "How good it is to see you again." Standing, he made an elaborate bow.

I curtseyed in return, hoping he could not see the tears on my face and the redness of my eyes. "Mr MacGillivray, I am surprised to see you here."

Baird waved his cheroot around vaguely. "There is no need for surprise, Miss Easson. After all, I am considering moving into the trading business. To do that I must inspect the docks to see what is happening. Pray, what brings you to this airt?"

"I was saying farewell to my intended," I said, surreptitiously wiping a tear with my gloved hand.

"Ah, of course. The good Mr Fairweather who sailed in *Admiral Duncan*." Baird revealed more knowledge than I had given him credit for. "Bound for the Kattegat and all points northeast."

"That's my man," I said.

"Well, as he's away, and you know you can trust me, perhaps you would not object to showing me around this dock? King William IV Dock, is it not?" Baird's smile wrapped around me.

"Mr MacGillivray," I said, "I have made it clear that I am engaged to Mr Fairweather."

"You have," Baird agreed.

"And although you stated that you wanted me for a wife, and have shown me nothing but kindness, I have no intention of altering my affections." I curtseyed again. "Besides, Mr MacGillivray, I have to get to work."

"Of course." Baird bowed. "May I be so bold as to ask where you work?"

I took a deep breath. "Blackwood's Mill," I informed him.

"Ah."

I doubted if Baird had ever been inside a mill, let alone spoken to a mill worker. It was an honest job, if poorly paid, but mill hands were low down the social order, often regarded as lesser people than the servants that men such as Baird MacGillivray had in such abundance.

"In that case," Baird said, giving a brief, possibly mocking, bow, "I shall leave you to your duties, and I shall have to continue without the pleasure of your company."

I did not know what pleasure a mill-girl's company could give to a gentleman, except the obvious, and he certainly was not getting that, so I hurried to the mill for another exhausting shift, with my mind filled with worry for our impending eviction, and sorrow for Kenneth's departure.

"Miss stuck-up is quiet today," Anne, one of my colleagues, nodded to me. I did not fit in with these, rough, hard-working, mainly good-hearted women, and Anne tried her best to capitalise on my isolation.

"She's always quiet," Isabel, her bosom companion said. "Never speaks to the likes of us."

I said nothing, with my mind frantically worrying how to pay the rent as well as thinking of Mother Faa's words about Kenny, and Baird's unexpected arrival at the docks.

"Look at her, standing there as if butter wouldn't melt in her mouth." Anne spoke in the high-pitched, rapid tones necessary to be heard above the constant clatter of the machinery.

I remained quiet, trying to ignore Anne as I worried myself sick about money. When we had our lunch half-hour, I screwed up my courage and approached the overseer, Mr Greer, a grey-faced, middle-aged man with eyes like flints.

"Yes?" Mr Greer snapped, glaring at me.

"I was wondering if I could work some extra hours," I said, "or have an advance of wages."

The flint-eyes sharpened into arrow-heads as they roamed the length of my body, as if the fingers of his mind were exploring me. I was always uncomfortable in the presence of Mr Greer. "Why?" he demanded.

"I need the money." I was not inclined to inform Mr Greer about my financial problems.

When Mr Green gave a sly grin, the expression of his eyes altered to something I liked even less. "I think we can come to an arrangement."

"Could you advance me wages?" I knew that if I used future wages to pay existing debt, I was delaying the problem rather than solving it. However, I had learned to live for the day and allow tomorrow to take care of itself.

"I can arrange extra hours," Mr Greer said, "with just you and me together, Miss Easson."

I stepped back quickly. "That is not the sort of arrangement I had in mind," I said.

"Are you behind in your rent? Is that it?" Mr Greer was well aware of the troubles that beset many families in Dundee. "Well, you may not be so high and mighty when you're out on the streets, Miss Easson."

I knew that was true. I would not be the first or the last woman to accept the advances of some repulsive man simply to keep a roof over my head. Prostitution was rife, and sometimes even the most respectable of women fell from grace to feed the family, or to keep from sleeping in the gutter.

"I will have to be desperate to accept you, Mr Greer," I responded, knowing that I was putting my position in jeopardy. I had been stupid even to approach such a blackguard and returned to my work feeling worse than ever.

I paid little attention to the coach standing outside the mill when I left work at seven that evening until the driver shouted my name.

"Miss Easson!"

I looked around, fully aware that half the spinners were doing likewise, with Anne nudging Isabel and pointing to me with some rude comment on her lips. I turned away, ignoring them.

Baird opened the door for me. "Good evening, Miss Easson." His smile was as broad as ever, with the late evening light reflecting from the signet ring on his little finger.

"Good evening, Mr MacGillivray." I gave a polite little curtsey, wishing he would leave me alone when all I wanted to do was hurry home and discuss our financial situation with my mother.

"Are you rushing again, Miss Easson?"

"I am going home, Mr MacGillivray."

"Then allow me to take you there." Baird threw open the door of the coach.

I hesitated, unsure what to do until the raucous voices of my workmates encouraged me to enter. "Go on, Catty," they called. "Take a ride with the gent!" There were other suggestions, but nothing that I can put on paper without a furious blush.

Aided by such advice, I boarded the carriage and, with my work companions hooting, we pulled away from the mill. It was only a short drive to Milne's Close.

"Here we are." I had travelled in silence, too overcome by financial worries to respond to Baird's conversation.

Now I had a decision to make. I could thank Baird for the use of his coach and leave, or I could invite him in. The first option would be impolite after his hospitality the previous day, while the second would introduce him to our poverty and probably shock him with the reality of our situation. Some devil took hold of me, and I decided on the latter course. I did not expect to see the man again, so what did it matter what he thought?

"Won't you come in?" I invited, hoping my mother would not mind.

"That is very kind of you," Baird accepted at once.

Leaving the coach in the Nethergate, I guided Baird down the narrow, unlit close and up the stairs to our house. Our steps echoed from the tall stone buildings as a neighbour peered from his doorway to see who was passing. I half-expected Baird to turn away at the darkness or scoff at the poverty, but instead he followed me, gave a cheerful greeting to our inquisitive neighbour and followed me in.

"I hope I don't ruin your reputation," Baird said.

"Oh, no, Mother will be inside the house," I told him, more in hope than anything else. "She finishes work an hour before I do."

Mother was indeed inside the house. I heard her sobbing as I pushed open the door.

"Mother!" Leaving poor Baird standing behind me, I knelt beside Mother, who sat at the table with her head in her arms.

"What's the matter?" Baird was all concern.

"Money." Mother sounded desperate. Her eyes were red with weeping. "Mr Milne is evicting us. I've seen him today to try and get him to give us more time, but he would not listen."

"Mother!" I exclaimed in horror. I did not like to discuss our money matters with other people. I had not even told Kenny our troubles. If Mother had been less distraught, she would not have mentioned our predicament at all.

"Why would he do that?" Baird looked around our house. I thought he might have mocked our poverty, but instead, he said. "Everything looks clean and tidy to me."

I sighed. "It's all right, Mr MacGillivray. We'll get by."

Baird was having none of it. Lifting Mr Milne's now-crumpled letter from the table, he scanned it in a single glance. "I see. May I have this?"

"It's all right, Mr MacGillivray," I insisted. "We'll sort it out."

Baird gave a little smile. "I happen to know Mr Milne," he said. "I might be able to help."

As I began to protest, Mother looked up, her face swollen with tears and her hands twisting a damp pocket-handkerchief into a long snake. "Could you do that, sir?"

"I most certainly could." Baird stilled any arguments I had by pocketing the letter.

"Mr MacGillivray," I said. "It's not right."

"Yesterday," Baird said, "you helped me. Today I shall help you. Or would you prefer that your mother remain distressed?"

I shook my head, knowing that Baird had struck me in my weakest spot. "I should not," I admitted.

"That's settled then," Baird said.

Mother stood up, looking older and wearier than I had ever seen her. "I have not even welcomed you in, sir."

"Your daughter did that most adequately," Baird, ever the perfect gentleman, gave a low bow. "I am honoured to meet you. Mrs Easson, isn't it?"

"That's correct." Mother looked nonplussed. "Thank you, sir."

"Now." Baird stepped back. "I know you have both had long days at work and wish to be left in peace, so I will not delay you."

I wondered why Baird had brought me to Milne's Close. "You've only just arrived," I protested. "I'll make some tea." Tea was my panacea for all situations.

"That would be most welcome, if it's not too much trouble." Baird gave another bow.

I checked our water supply, for we bought it by the bucketful from the water-carriers, found we had plenty left, so it was the work of five minutes to fill the kettle and light the fire. "It won't be long," I said.

"Catriona makes good strong tea," Mother said. I could see her eyeing Baird curiously, clearly wondering who he was. Since the sea claimed Father, she had good days when she was as healthy as she had always been, and bad days, when she seemed to exist in a daze of uncertainty. The threat of eviction had pushed her into one of the latter, and I silently cursed Mr Milne.

"Strong tea is my preference, too," Baird said.

Mother's smile was good to see.

I saw Baird's eyes narrow as he focussed on the shelves of books that lined one wall of the room. He looked at me, and then at Mother. "I believe you work in a shop, Mrs Easson and Miss Easson works in a mill."

"That's correct," Mother agreed.

Baird nodded. "Is it usual for ladies in these occupations to have shelves of books and read the newspaper? Excuse my inquisitiveness." Standing, he perused our books, reading out the authors. "Walter Scott, Byron, Wordsworth, Tacitus?" He looked around with his eyebrows raised. "Your reading material is interesting."

I said nothing. I had always read; my father encouraged us to read.

"Are such books normal for mill workers?" Baird repeated his question. "And can many mill workers converse sensibly in educated company, as Miss Easson did yesterday?" His gaze roamed further around the room until it stopped at our chess set. "Or play chess?"

"I don't know what is usual," I replied. "We are all individuals."

Baird nodded, smiling. "None of my concern, then." He glanced at me before addressing my mother. "Mrs Easson, I wish to ask your daughter to a ball at the Provost's House."

"Oh, sir." Mother glanced from Baird to me and back.

I said nothing at this surprising news. I had never thought to see Baird again, despite his professed intention to marry me. I had certainly never expected him to ask me to a ball, and the Provost's Ball was one of the highlights of Dundee's social season, not an occasion to which a mill-girl could ever aspire to attend.

"Will you come to the ball with me, Miss Easson? I suspect you have been to a ball before and will have the appropriate clothing hidden away."

I stiffened, wondering what else this perceptive man knew about us, or guessed about us, or thought he knew about us. "I am afraid I cannot come," I said. I knew I sounded churlish after Baird had offered to speak to Mr Milne. "I am not ungrateful for the offer, Mr MacGillivray, and I am sensible of the great honour you do me, but I am engaged to Mr Fairweather and would not abuse his friendship."

"Of course, I understand your reasons," Baird gave another graceful bow. "However, I shall miss your company."

"No, Catriona," Mother sounded more like herself again. "Mr MacGillivray has offered to help us out of our current financial predicament. The least you can do is accept his kind request and accompany him to the ball."

"Kenneth might not agree," I protested.

"Kenneth might never know." Mother managed a small smile. "I can't see any of his seafaring men attending the Provost's Ball, and you deserve some pleasure, Catriona. Life has been hard recently."

"You are a wise woman, Mrs Easson," Baird said with perfect solemnity.

"I know that you will be a perfect gentleman," Mother added, with more than a hint of steel in her voice.

"I can assure you of that," Baird said.

So that was how I found myself, a spinner at Blackwood's Mill going to the Provost's Ball with Mr Baird MacGillivray of Mysore House.

~

The ball, I found out, was not for some four weeks, giving me sufficient time to get myself prepared. Naturally, all my workmates at the mill were eager to hear who the gentleman in the coach had been.

"Is that your young man?" They asked. "Is that Kenneth Fairweather?"

Anne glowered at me through poisonous eyes. "That wasn't a seafaring man, not with a coach and horses."

"That was Mr Baird MacGillivray," I said. "He's not a friend, only an acquaintance."

"He must like you," Anne said. "And he's wealthy to have a coach such as that." She gave what was meant to be a coy smile. "Maybe you should drop your sailor friend and go with him." Her once-pretty face creased into a frown. "Baird MacGillivray? Is that not the fellow from Mysore House?"

"That's the man," I said, wishing that they would get their long noses out of my business. But gossip was the lifeblood of the mills, although we worked non-stop with our voices high pitched above the clatter of machinery.

"He's rich." Anne emphasised her words. "The family made their money in Hindustan." She raised her voice so everybody close by could hear. "They have a hundred servants in their house and worship an Indian god. They have pet snakes and lions to keep their servants under control."

"Do they?" I responded, all wide-eyed innocence. I did not tell Anne that I had been inside Mysore House. Anne was not the sort of person to whom one revealed confidences.

"I heard that old man MacGillivray married a blackie," Anne said. "The master bought her at a market in China and brought her back as a slave, so that means your sweetheart is half-Indian." She nodded to herself. "Aye, I thought so when I saw him outside the mill. That's a foreigner, I thought, coming to kidnap us and take us all to Hindustan."

"He can take me any time, with a coach like that," commented Mag Dodds. Mags was middle-aged and prematurely grey, with a kindly eye. "Indeed, he can take me any time – even without his coach." She led the raucous laughter.

"He has already taken Catriona, I wager," Anne said. "Isn't that right, Catty? He's taken you in the way men like to take women!"

"He has not!" I denied, so hotly that the women nudged themselves in amusement.

"So you say," Anne looked around, gathering support. "What do you think, girls?"

Some laughed, some concentrated on their work. Mag Dodds winked at me across the clattering machinery, but a few added cruel comments to Anne's words. I was not the most popular worker in that mill, with my different background and tastes.

"I wonder what your sailor will say when he hears about your antics with that Indian prince." Anne continued her attack.

"There were no antics," I said. "And he's not an Indian prince."

"Says you," Anne sneered, nudging her neighbour. "Says her, eh?" She glowered at me in suspicion. "I know you think you're better than us common mill lassies, with you speaking like you've got a bool in your mouth."

"Aye," a gaunt-faced woman agreed. "I seen her reading the paper, too, like she wanted to be one of the nobs."

I said nothing. I did not feel superior to any of the mill girls. I knew I was no better than them, even if I did read the newspaper and could play chess. I had not enjoyed my working days at the mill before I met Baird, and I enjoyed them even less when I became the object of Anne's barbed humour. Sometimes I stood there in grim silence, at other times my angry reaction let Anne know her attacks were successful and brought me to the overseer's attention. Mr Greer had not forgiven me for repulsing his advances and he began to watch me closely, checking everything I did and looking for faults.

With Kenny at sea and taunts at work, I was not happy for the next few weeks, as the days ticked away to the ball. However, one major source of discontent ended when Mr Milne sent his factor to our house.

The heavy knock at the door sounded like death coming to visit.

Mother was having one of her bad days and looked up fearfully. "Go and answer that," she said, hunched in the chair she seldom left when she was at home. "It might be the minister." The irregular visits of Mr Grieve, the minister, were the only high points of Mother's life, possibly because both had recently lost their spouses and understood one another's anguish.

It was not Mr Grieve. Instead, it was Mr Graham the factor, standing there with the usual sour expression on his skull-like face and his ice-chip eyes as friendly as Bonaparte's brother. "Yes, Mr Graham?" I said, standing in the doorway with my heart hammering with nervousness, yet determined to block his access. Ever since father's death, Mother had been unable to cope with officialdom in any form. I had dreaded a visit from Mr Graham since the day we received notice of eviction.

"I was expecting to evict you two," Mr Graham stated, trying to peer past me to see the interior of the house.

"Oh?" I kept my voice non-committal.

"I see that will no longer be necessary," Mr Graham said. "Your rent has been paid in full."

Thank you, Baird MacGillivray, I thought. I had wondered if he would keep his word. Now I had to attend the Provost's Ball and hoped that Kenny would understand. I cannot express the relief that Mr Graham's one statement gave me. It was like a massive weight removed from my back.

"You seem to have made an influential friend." Mr Graham tipped forward his low-brimmed hat and tapped the end of his cane on the stone flags of the close. "Mr Snodgrass tells me you had a man to the house." Snodgrass was our prying neighbour.

I said nothing, hoping Graham would leave soon. Men such as Graham always left me feeling dirty, as if I had associated with the devil or one of his minions. I needed a visit to the kirk, for the dirt was more of the spirit as the body.

"Your influential friend paid your rent for the next three months." Graham continued to try to look inside the house as he spoke. "Now, why would he do that?"

I remained static, determined not to give him an inch of leeway. *Thank you, even more, Baird MacGillivray.* With three months' rent paid in advance, we had breathing space to set our finances in order. I determined to be as nice as I could to Baird at the ball. I might even begin to like that enigmatic, charming man. Mother Faa's words came to me again: "This man will help you see your Kenny as he truly is," and, "Choose carefully."

"In that case, Mr Graham," I said, "I can see no reason for your being here. We have no arrears and no debts. Thank you for telling me." I would have closed the door on him had he not thrust his foot in the door.

"Not quite yet, Miss Easson." Mr Graham's face would have chilled the fires of Hades and sent the devil himself squealing for help. "It is a condition of your lease that you do nothing of a non-respectable nature." Graham rapped his cane against the jamb of the door. "I wish to enter your house."

"Why?" I asked, although I was beginning to understand what Graham meant.

"Women who can suddenly pay advance rent when they are only making a spinner's wage must have another source of income."

Although I remained still, my temper rose. "What are you insinuating, Mr Graham?"

"I believe you are running a disorderly house, Miss Easson." For the first time, Graham smiled, and such a smile I hope never to see again. I did not intend to slap him, I really did not, but I have seldom felt such satisfaction as I did when I sent him staggering.

"Get out!" I said as my temper took control of my good sense. I stepped forward, ready to hit him again as he gripped his cane, straightened his hat and glowered at me.

"Mr Milne will hear about this."

"Good," I said. "You may tell Mr Milne that I do not appreciate being insulted by his minions." I shut the door with a bang, shaking with a mixture of anger and apprehension, for Mr Graham was an unpleasant man. Even with our rent paid in advance, Graham could stir up trouble or persuade Mr Milne to evict us. As my temper cooled, I began to regret that slap, however delicious it had been.

Mother looked up with that horrible vacant look back in her eyes. "What was that all about?"

"Nothing for you to concern yourself about," I said. "Mr Baird MacGillivray has paid our rent for the next few months."

"Oh, that is very kind of him," Mother said. "Why did he do that?"

"I am not sure," I replied, truthfully.

"I wonder if he is tipping his hat at you," Mother said.

"He knows I am spoken for." I wished I had never met Baird, even although he had eased our financial burden. No, I told myself, that was a foolish thing to think. If Baird had not paid our rent, we would be living in the streets by now, or, if we were fortunate, sharing a room with a dozen men and women in some crumbling lodging house in Couttie's Wynd or some other place of ill repute.

Mother's smile reminded me of happier times when Father was home from sea. "Kenneth Fairweather is a solid young man, Catriona, but you're not married yet. A cat can look at a queen, remember, and an unmarried woman can alter her affection if a better man happens along."

"Baird is not a better man than Kenny," I said.

"Are you accompanying Mr MacGillivray to the Provost's Ball?" Mother asked sweetly.

"Yes." I made my final decision. "Yes, I am."

Mother's smile wrapped around me. "I am glad to hear it, Catriona. Baird will be an excellent catch for you."

"I don't want to catch him," I insisted. "I already have Kenny in my net."

"Choose carefully." I shivered as Mother's words echoed those of Mother Faa.

"I already have," I said. Or I thought I had. Now I was not so sure.

It was three days before somebody else knocked at our door. Taking a deep breath, I eased it open to find Mr Milne himself standing there. He took his tall hat off. "Miss Easson," he greeted me, giving a small bow.

"Mr Milne," I waited for his pronouncement of doom. Slapping his factor no longer seemed like a good idea.

"May I come in?"

Although I had no qualms about facing up to the factor, Mr Milne owned our house, and indeed the rest of the close. I stepped aside with as much good grace as I could muster and ushered him inside.

"Do sit down, Mr Milne." Mother was more herself that day. She pulled up a chair for Mr Milne. I leaned against the bookshelves, wondering where we would spend the night.

"Ah, this is slightly awkward." Mr Milne was middle aged with more white than grey in his whiskers and inclined to a portly figure. "I believe that Miss Easson recently had words with Mr Graham."

"I did." I waited for the axe to fall. I had an instant vision of the future: immediate eviction and a home on the streets with nights spent huddled in shop doorways and the contempt of the more fortunate citizens of Dundee. "I slapped his face for him."

Milne held his hat on his lap. "I can only apologise for the behaviour of my factor," he said.

I nearly collapsed with relief and surprise, stooping to lift three books that I dislodged from the shelves. "Mr Graham accused us of running a house of ill-repute," I said.

Mr Milne closed his eyes. "It is even worse than I thought," he said. "I will speak to Mr Graham and ensure such a thing never happens again."

"Thank you," I said with my mind in utter turmoil.

"Do you wish a dish of tea, Mr Milne?" Mother asked.

"No, no, thank you. I will not detain you further," Milne said. "I only wished to apologise." His hesitation was uncharacteristic. "I would be obliged if word of this unfortunate occurrence does not reach Mr MacGillivray's ears."

"The occurrence is closed," I assured him solemnly, enjoying Mr Milne's discomfiture. "As far as we are concerned, Mr MacGillivray will hear nothing about it."

"Thank you." Mr Milne rose, still holding his hat in both hands. "I would like to have been a witness to your meeting with Mr Graham," he said. "He is a very officious fellow if a very efficient factor."

"He is an insufferable blackguard," I said cheerfully.

When Mr Milne replaced his hat on his head, I was sure there was a glint of humour in his eyes. "Quite so, Miss Easson, quite so. Well, I will take up no more of your time."

"What on earth was that about?" Mother asked when I closed the door on Mr Milne's retreating back.

"I'm not sure," I said. "I think Baird MacGillivray might have something to do with it."

"How kind," Mother said. "We'd better find you something suitable to wear for the Provost's Ball."

"It is a masque ball," I said. "We have to come in some costume from the past, wearing a mask to disguise our identities."

Mother smiled. "Well now, Catriona, that is all to the good. We may not have much money or any position, but we are both good needlewomen, and I know others who will help. Now, all we have to decide is what costume you wish to wear." She looked at me through the corners of her eyes. "Something a leetle revealing I think, for Mr Baird MacGillivray. I suspect he is the sort of man who could be influenced by something a trifle risqué!"

"Mother!" I was genuinely shocked. "I will not be displaying myself for Baird's titillation."

"Oh, no Catriona," Mother replied. "You won't be displaying yourself for Baird MacGillivray. You'll be displaying yourself for Catriona Easson. One must make use of every advantage one has." Her smile was as calculating as that of any businessman making a deal. "A woman's beauty does not last for ever, Catriona. Think of yourself as an apple; the flesh of an apple is attractive but it is the pips that matter. In women, it is the soul and heart that matter but our outside appearance attracts men. We have to make the best catch we can while we're young, and if we don't have money and land, we must use our other assets – our looks."

I shook my head. "I've never heard you talk like this before, Mother."

"You're getting no younger, Catriona. You're 25 now. Unless you marry soon, you'll be too old and left on the shelf. I thought that Kenneth Fairweather would have married you by now, but it seems he is too hesitant. God has offered you a second chance with Baird MacGillivray, and when God opens a door for you, you should not slam it in his face."

I nodded, for I could see Mother's point of view. Once again, Mother Faa's image came before me.

"Now, all we have to do is create a costume that enhances your curves without destroying your reputation." Mother patted my hip, smiling.

CHAPTER 5

DUNDEE, MAY 1827

I had not known what to expect that night. Provost Thomas Bell held his ball in a detached house in the wealthier western section of the Nethergate, with half the great and the good of Dundee and surroundings attending. Baird had picked me up in his carriage, and we drove to the entrance in grand style, with the footmen in fancy dark-green-and-gold livery and the matching horses as gleaming as the coachwork of the chariot.

I took a deep breath as the coach pulled up outside the Provost's house.

"Now don't be nervous," Baird said. "You are with me. If anybody says anything untoward, they will have me to answer to." His smile never faltered.

"Why are you doing this?" I asked. "Why are you being so kind to me?"

Baird shook his head. "Because I like you," he said.

I did not understand. Certainly, I was not unsightly, but neither was I anybody's idea of a great beauty and I had nothing in common with a gentleman and merchant such as Baird MacGillivray.

"You are doing far too much merely because I chanced upon you when your chariot was in a ditch," I said.

"We both know there is far more to you than that, Miss Easson." Baird shook his head. "When you are ready, we can drop the pretence." He eyed me up and down, lingering on the places where Mother had cleverly emphasised my natural shape. "You look enchanting."

"I am supposed to be the Lady of the Lake." I should have posed for him at that point, but natural shyness forbade such a movement. "The enchantress who gave Excalibur to King Arthur."

"Ah," Baird smiled. My costume was as simple as it could be, a single white robe that showed enough of my bosom to tantalise without being indecent. Mother had spent hours getting just the right balance. "You are enchanting, indeed. Come, Miss Easson." Baird bowed and presented his arm. He was dressed in an old-fashioned costume as the Scarlet Pimpernel, a fictitious character who helped free aristocratic prisoners from the French Revolutionaries. Despite myself, I could not help admiring him, with his close-fitting breeches that emphasised his elegant legs and the immaculate silk shirt that revealed his breadth of chest. I looked away hurriedly when I realised we were each admiring the other in a manner that was not quite respectable.

"I'm coming," I said, wishing I was anywhere but there. I resolved that, whatever Baird had done for Mother and me in the past, I would break off our friendship as soon as this ball was over. I felt a fraud for acting as a companion to Baird when I knew I was not. Kenny was at sea, braving storms and ice, and here I was, cavorting with some man I barely knew.

"You will enchant more than me tonight, Miss Easson," Baird said. He looked around the crowd that waited to enter the house. "You're more beautiful than any of the women here."

"Oh!" I was not used to compliments. Kenny was not a man who gave accolades easily, if at all. "Thank you." I struggled to find a suitable response. "You are too fulsome in your praise, sir, and you look very handsome yourself." *Should I have said that? Oh, Lord, was I following the path of easy virtue? Oh, please help me to do what is right!*

Baird's bow was response enough. "Pray take my arm," he said.

I laid my hand lightly on the crook of his elbow and allowed him to guide me to the front door where a tall footman in an elaborate 18th-century costume announced us.

"Mr Baird MacGillivray of Mysore House and Miss Catriona Easson of Nethergate."

Heads turned to look at us, with both women and men concentrating on Baird, for Mysore House was something of a mystery to the good citizens of Dundee. Some women examined me critically, no doubt noting that my costume was home-made and my shape more homely than elegant.

"Mask up," Baird murmured, and I thankfully shielded my face. "Here comes the Provost."

Provost Bell was in his late fifties, a short-haired, pouch-faced man with a hard mouth and his right eye larger than his left. In common with many of the town's elite, he was a merchant and flax-spinner, more used to searching for a profit than entertaining at a ball. Dressed like a Scottish Napoleon Bonaparte, he glanced at me and bowed without interest.

"Miss Easson."

"Provost Bell." I gave him a perfunctory curtsey.

"Mr MacGillivray." Bell faced Baird directly. "I believe you intend to invest in the trade of Dundee."

"That is so," Baird said.

"I can help you make decisions," Bell said.

"I have heard you are an astute businessman," Baird agreed, "and I will certainly consult with you on a future occasion." Producing a card from somewhere within his costume, Baird handed it over. "My card, sir."

"And mine." Bonaparte-Bell bowed again, said, "Your servant, ma'am," to me and moved stiffly away.

"As you see," Baird murmured. "These occasions are not all about pleasure. It allows one to mingle with fellow businessmen in a more amenable setting and see who is making deals with whom." He grinned at me. "It also enables the fair ones to gather sufficient gossip to enliven their lives. They will spend the next week smiling sweetly as they destroy the character of their dearest friends."

I forced a smile, although I had no desire to put myself in a position for vicious women to hone their claws on my character.

"You'll know all about such things of course," Baird said casually. "This will not be the first ball you have attended."

"I have been to similar gatherings." I thought of the celebrations to which Father had taken me to when the Baltic season ended, and ship owners and shipmasters gathered together. "Not quite like this, though."

"No." Baird bowed to a passing woman dressed as Marie Antoinette. I wondered why so many people were interested in that bitter period of history and dismissed the thought. "No, you'll be used to mingling with a higher stratum of society."

"Hardly that!" My laugh was genuine as I compared the rough-hewn seamen with these elegantly-mannered gentlemen and ladies.

"You are indeed an intriguing lady," Baird said. "You and I shall have the most interesting conversations."

"Why, thank you, sir." I gave a mock curtsey. "I am just myself and hardly of interest to anybody." As I spoke, I thought of my monosyllabic Kenny and wondered if I could ever hold an interesting conversation with him, or indeed, any discussion that lasted more than two minutes.

Baird's smile dropped as he surveyed me. "I find that hard to believe, Miss Easson. I think that a woman such as you would interest any man, whatever his social status." His eyes were serious for a moment and then laughed again. "Come, Miss Easson, the ball is the poorer for our absence."

I looked inside the house where a crowd of people in every sort of dress and costume were curious to see the elusive Pimpernel of

Mysore House. My presence, I knew, was only an extra. The women, in particular, looked interested in Baird, with some openly eyeing him up and down and retiring to make polite conversation to their friends. As Baird's companion, I came in for a little attention, but when people realised that I was not from their class, they shunned me with cold shoulders and frozen stares.

"Baird MacGillivray has brought one of his servant girls with him, I see." A tall red-head dressed as Aphrodite looked over her shoulder at me.

"Oh no, Jennifer; she's a mill-girl, I believe." A blonde who threatened to burst free of her over-tight Maid Marian costume gave me a poisonous look. I said nothing but wondered what had given her the idea that Marian had decorated her clothes with a plethora of ribbons.

"Oh, how charming of Mr MacGillivray." Aphrodite replaced her mask. "He must be the most condescending of men. Does he have money, do you know?"

"Oh, piles of it," Maid Marian said. I wondered what my fellow mill workers would think of her, with her skirt so short that only her ribbons kept her decent.

This class system we have is a terrible thing, where people refuse to mix with anyone from a different social background. Were it not for Baird, I should have been alone in that house, among all these people. However, I knew that Mother would be a fountain of questions, so I observed all I could, ignored the more pointed of rebuffs and held my temper in check.

"Shall we dance?" Baird invited as the small band began to play a waltz.

I knew the rudiments, nothing more, for the coasters' annual gatherings do not prepare one for mixing with the Provost and elite of Dundee's society. Luckily Baird was as accomplished at dancing as he seemed to be at everything else, so I followed his lead and managed to finish the waltz without making a complete fool of myself. I noticed Baird glancing at Maid Marian as we stepped around her.

"Is that not the woman who was insulting you?" he enquired.

"One of them," I said. "It doesn't matter."

"It matters to me," Baird's mouth was tight. "I did not invite you here to be insulted by some ill-mannered woman from a minor trading family. He winked. "Watch this."

I could not see precisely what Baird did, although I suspect he looped one of Marian's ribbons over his foot. Suddenly I heard a shrill squeal and whirled round to see Marian stagger and fall face first, bending at the waist so that her minuscule skirt lifted above her waist, the ribbons parted on either side and her plump rump thrust upwards.

"Are you all right?" Baird was the first to straighten Marian up.

I heard small sounds of laughter from the other guests, with Aphrodite to the fore.

"You poor thing." I added my contribution to Marian's discomfort. "That must have been terribly embarrassing for you, to end in such a revealing position."

"Oh." Maid Marian brushed down her ribbons in a belated attempt to restore her dignity.

As Marian stamped away in a fine huff, I found Baird at my side.

"You did that deliberately," I hissed.

"I know," Baird agreed at once. "It was rather fun, wasn't it? I'll be back shortly." He guided me to a seat. "Now you behave yourself until I come back."

I sat in silence, wishing I had not come as the crowd milled about me, speaking in accents so refined I could hardly understand them. Every time I heard a laugh, I was sure they were talking about me until somebody eventually addressed me directly.

"Are you the woman with Mr Baird MacGillivray?"

I looked up. The speaker had deliberately and pointedly used the term "woman" to emphasise that I was no lady. "I am with Baird," I said.

"Oh." She looked down her long nose at me, a tall, elegant piece, supremely confident in her superiority over everybody she happened to meet. "Who are you?"

"Catriona Easson." I kept my voice pleasant. "Who are you?"

"I am Miss Clarissa Ogilvy of Pitlunie."

I nodded, unsure what to say.

"Are you anybody?" Miss Clarissa Ogilvy held her mask in her hand.

"Just myself," I was fully aware she was probing to find out my status, wealth and background.

Clarissa Ogilvy pursed her lips. "I see." She looked up when Baird came back. "Oh, Mr MacGillivray." She swooped in an elegant curtsey that somehow exposed her well-proportioned cleavage to his view. Honestly, behind closed doors, these women of a supposedly superior class really were the most awful trollops. "I am so pleased to make your acquaintance. I have been talking to your most delightful companion here. She is a most interesting woman."

Baird bowed in return. "Have you met Miss Catriona before, Miss..? I am sorry. I do not know your name."

"I am Miss Clarissa Ogilvy of Pitlunie."

"Oh." Baird gave a little frown, which was most unlike him. "Pitlunie. No, I am sorry, Miss Clarissa, I am afraid I know of no such place." He turned to me with another bow. "Do you know of Pitlunie, Your Ladyship?"

I started until I realised that Baird was playing Miss Clarissa at her own game. "Mr MacGillivray!" I tapped his arm gently with my mask. "I told you not to call me that!"

I saw by the twinkle in Baird's eye that he appreciated my retort. "I do apologise, Your... Miss Easson. I had quite forgotten." His bow was so low I feared his trousers would split, which would have been interesting for me, if embarrassing for him. Although Baird, being the man he was, could have passed over even such a calamity with a smile and some smooth words.

"Oh." Miss Clarissa looked at Baird and then at me. I swear she turned white. "I do apologise, Your Ladyship," she said. "I had no idea."

"You are correct," I replied. "You have no idea." Turning my head as if in disdain, I began a conversation with Baird, choosing Indian politics as a subject about which Miss Clarissa would hopefully know even less than I did. From the corner of my eye, I saw her walk away with just the slightest slope of her shoulders to show her discomfiture.

"Thank you, Mr MacGillivray," I said when Miss Clarissa was out of our hearing. "That was kind of you. Indeed, that is twice that you have intervened on my behalf."

"You are more important to me than Miss Clarissa Ogilvy," Baird said. "I have met her kind before, women who think they are important because they have come into money, while you..." He stepped back and looked at me. "You are a genuine lady."

"I am only a mill girl," I said. "The daughter of a sailor."

Baird laughed. "Of course; I had quite forgotten who you said you were." He presented his hand. "Shall we dance, Miss Easson?"

We danced again, with Miss Clarissa Ogilvy sulking after her rebuff and the music circling in my head. That night still lives in my memory as a whirl of colour and pleasure and an insight into the lives of the elite of Dundee, where money was no object, and nobody had to balance paying the rent with feeding the family; there was sufficient money for both and much left over. I also remember that night as a time when I saw the kindness of Baird MacGillivray and the manner in which he defended me from women to whose barbed jibes I was insufficiently experienced to reply. After the retreat of Miss Ogilvy, nobody else, woman or man, cared to address me in anything except favourable terms, although I am not sure whether that was due to Baird's presence, or the rumour that I was some titled lady in disguise. After all, it was a masked ball, and we all hid behind some form of dissimulation.

My head was whirling when I left Nethergate House, with music and laughter jostling together with all the colour and joy of the ball. I sat back in the coach, humming the waltz tunes, smiling at my memories and wishing I was starting the entire evening all over again. After a few moments, I realised that the driver was not taking us towards Milne's Close. "Where are we heading?" I asked.

"Mysore House," Baird told me. "Only for a few moments and then I'll take you home."

I did not object. I was growing rather used to travelling in style and moving with the elite of society. It would be hard to return to our little house, to the penny-pinching poverty that was our lot.

Within a few moments, we rolled up the now-familiar drive of Mysore House, and a footman opened the carriage door. Baird leaned towards me. "Would you prefer to remain in the carriage, Miss Easson? Or would you care to wait in the house."

"Oh, I'll come inside," I said, slightly careless of my words. I allowed the footman to help me down the small step and nearly danced inside Mysore House, still humming the waltz.

"Come up to the first floor." Baird seemed happy with my choice. "Shall I find something for you to drink?"

"No thank you," I said, responding to a maid's curtsey with one of my own and following Baird up the carpeted staircase, softly singing.

I waited into one of the front rooms but, unable to sit still, I waltzed myself around on the Persian carpet, manoeuvring around the furniture and ensuring I did not make contact with the glass-fronted bookcase. The curtains at the east-facing window were half-open and the shutters not yet closed so I peered outside at the grounds, wondering what it would be like to be mistress of such an establishment. What sort of life would I lead if I allowed Baird to follow through on his idea of making me his wife? The thought made me smile until I saw the people moving outside the house. There were two of them at the very fringe of the arc of light thrown by Mysore House, and I knew them both.

One was Barbara, Baird's beautiful but ill-humoured sister, and the other was my very own Kenny. I stopped my dancing at once, stepped aside and stared at them from the shelter of the curtains as my erstwhile happy mood plummeted into despair.

The shapely Barbara was standing so close to Kenny that they were almost touching, and they were talking together. Feeling sick, I could only watch as my man lost himself in Barbara's evident charms and the life I had planned shattered like cheap crockery dropped on a stone-flagged floor. After a few moments, they moved slightly, still deeply engaged in whatever they were discussing. The light reflected on something in Kenny's hand, something that glittered and sparkled.

A piece of jewellery.

Kenny had given Barbara a piece of jewellery. It must be a ring.

I had known Kenny since childhood, and in all that time he had never given me as much as a smooth farthing. Yet here he was handing over jewellery to Barbara and, to judge by his sea-clothes, he was fresh from *Admiral Duncan*. In my experience, there was only one reason for an unmarried man to give a ring to an unmarried woman. Kenny, my monosyllabic Kenny, my long-term intended, had also proposed to Barbara MacGillivray.

I turned away, choking on my tears. After all the emotion I had wasted on that man, he had rushed from his ship to see this woman with a ring he must have purchased in foreign parts.

Suddenly all the good feelings from the ball dissipated. I stood in that most lovely room with the music dying in my head and the steady ticking of the clock like a countdown to the end of days.

"Miss Easson?"

At the sound of Baird's voice, I stepped back and allowed the curtain to fall back into place, blocking the view of the scene outside. I turned with a forced smile on my face. "Yes, Mr MacGillivray?"

Baird's expression altered. "Are you all right, Miss Easson? You look as pale as if you'd seen a ghost." He stepped forward, all masculine concern as he put his hand on my arm.

I broadened my smile, knowing it must appear like a death's head grin. "I'm all right," I said.

"Has it been too much for you?" Baird sounded genuinely concerned. "Did the ball continue too late for you? I should have taken you straight home rather than coming here first. I do apologise;

I wished to pick up something." He shook his head. "It was unforgivable of me."

"It's not that," I said, comparing Baird's apology with the heartlessness of the man with whom I hoped to share my life. I took a deep breath and tried to control my emotions, giving a curtsey to hide my pain. "You have always been a perfect gentleman, Mr MacGillivray. I could not have asked for a more consummate escort."

I think Baird's smile was genuine. "Thank you, Miss Easson."

"And now, sir," I struggled with my tears. "I should be obliged if you could take me home."

"Your chariot awaits," Baird announced, opening the door with a flourish.

I walked out, half-hoping to meet Kenny and have it out with him, and half-hoping to avoid him until I had my emotions under control. If I had met him, I do not know how I would have reacted. I might have burst into tears in front of everybody, or thrown myself at him in a fury, which would have been quite as bad. As it happened, our passage out of Mysore House was without incident, and I sat in the coach wondering what the future might hold.

"Have you enjoyed your evening, Miss Easson?" Baird asked.

"I enjoyed it very much, Mr MacGillivray." I touched his arm. "You are too kind to me."

"You say you enjoyed the evening, Miss Easson," Baird said, "yet your eyes give the lie."

"I enjoyed the evening with you, Mr MacGillivray," I said. "And now I would like to go home."

"Can you tell me why there is such sadness in your eyes?"

I had to disguise the tears that were only a blink away, so I leaned closer to Baird. "I shall give you this instead," I said and kissed him, gently, on the cheek. His skin was soft and slightly scented.

Baird touched his cheek. "I shall treasure that kiss as the first you granted me," he said. "May I be permitted to return the favour?"

I thought again of Kenny's treachery with Barbara. "It is little enough reward for all your kindness." I presented my face for his lips.

Leaning forward, Baird pressed his lips softly against my forehead. "There now," he said. "A kiss for a kiss, a smile for a smile and my heart is open for you."

"Thank you," I said as I stumbled out of the coach with my emotions in confusion. "Thank you, Mr MacGillivray."

I did not ask Baird to accompany me into our house for by that time I could no longer control the hot tears that blinded me as I wondered what I should do about Kenny.

CHAPTER 6

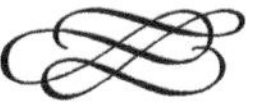

DUNDEE, MAY 1827

Mother was not so unsure about my future.

"Well now," she said when I sobbed out my story and sat at the table in passive, damp-faced misery. "It seems as if Master Kenneth Fairweather has been leading a false life with you."

I nodded, wordless and with no tears left in me.

"I never liked that man," Mother said, in complete contrast to her usual declarations of Kenny's sterling qualities.

I nodded, not caring about her inconsistencies.

"I'd like to do something about him," Mother said. "I'd like a stern word with that sailor."

Strangely, I was perversely pleased to hear my mother in such a taking. Ever since father had died, she had been listless, working without enthusiasm and unemotionally accepting anything that life threw at us. Now, with her daughter slighted, she had recovered some of her old spirit. I was not quite ready to thank Kenny for being a mountebank, but I cannot think what else could have so effectively shifted the darkness from Mother's mood.

"I'll speak to him later," I said. "I'd better get to bed. I have work tomorrow. You too, Catriona. You have tasted the finer side of life and learned of your intended's fickleness. That is enough for one night, and life must go on. Despite Mr MacGillivray's kindness in paying our bills, we still have to earn money."

"Yes, Mother," I agreed.

"Come." Mother patted my shoulder. "It is not as bad as it could be. You have discovered the truth before the marriage. Can you imagine how much worse it would be if Kenneth Fairweather had acted in such a manner after you were married and it was too late to do anything about it?"

I nodded, although, at that time, the thought was little consolation. I raised my head as I got myself under control. "That is true, Mother," I said. "No wonder Barbara and I had disliked each other at first sight; she must have known that she was taking Kenny from me."

"Now that you have that settled in your mind," Mother said, "you can concentrate on your other young man." Her eyes were no longer vacant as she held me. "Put Kenneth Fairweather away," Mother urged, "and concentrate on Mr Baird MacGillivray."

I took that thought to bed with me, yet it was Kenny's open face that taunted me as my tears dampened the pillow.

Naturally, with Dundee being more like a large village than a town, word had spread about the ball and my presence there. Anne was ready to torment me the moment I stepped inside Blackwood's Mill.

"Here she comes, little miss stuck-up, too good to talk to the likes of us."

Greer, the overseer, stomped over, smelling of stale beer from his excesses the previous night. "Well, she'd better be prepared to work for me," he said. "Or she'll feel my belt across her shoulders."

"There's no need for that, Mr Greer," Mag Dodds said. "Catriona is as good a worker as any in the mill."

"Is she?" Mr Greer patted the heavy leather strap that hung at his waist. "There's always trouble when she's around."

"She's a grown woman, and no child to be beaten," Mag Dodds supported me.

Mr Greer sneered at me. "That's for me to decide."

Keeping my head down, I worked in silence as Anne threw insult after insult at me, trying to provoke a response.

"That MacGillivray man can't like you for yourself," Anne jeered "You've nothing for a man like him. You must be giving him something he wants in return for taking you to the Provost's Ball." She looked around her followers. "We all know what that is, don't we, girls?"

I said nothing, thinking of Kenny's betrayal, wanting to take out my humiliation and anger on Anne and knowing I could not.

"Leave Catty alone – you're stirring a wasps' nest, Anne." Mag Dodds could see the expression on my face. "Best leave her alone."

"I will not leave her." Anne revelled in my unhappiness. "She deserves it." Leaning across the machinery, she put her mouth close to my ear and spat: "She must be acting the whore."

I knew we needed any money that I could bring home, but I was already in a fragile state, and Anne's last insult cracked my always-frail patience. Leaving the loom to run itself, I ran to retaliate, only for Anne's colleagues to take her part. So, within a few moments, I was on the receiving end of a drubbing. I struck back of course but was not winning when Greer came to break up the stramash with oaths and much muscle power.

"What's to do?" He demanded, pressing his beery face against mine.

I said nothing as Anne, and her colleagues give their version of events, with me cast as the villain and themselves as innocent angels. The overseer listened, smiled and motioned to me. "I'll take you to the manager, Miss Troublemaker Easson, and you'll be out of here before you can say goodbye."

With the overseer's hand gripping my shoulder, I walked to the manager's office, seething with frustrated anger. *Now I've lost my position as well as my man. What can I tell Mother?* I wondered.

"Name?" Mr Thoms, the manager, was a middle-aged grey man and looked at me through indifferent eyes. He was interested only in getting his work done and thought of his workers merely as pawns, bodies needed for the job rather than women with hopes, feelings and dreams.

"Catriona Easson," I replied wearily, wondering how much worse my life could get. I did not expect compassion or fairness.

"What?" The manager started. "Catriona Easson?" He looked at me as if I were something different. "Do you happen to know Mr Baird MacGillivray?" he asked.

"Yes," I said. *Was this man going to hold that against me as well?*

The silence was palpable as Mr Thoms stared at me in horror as if unable to decide what to do, or what a gentleman such as Mr MacGillivray could see in such an unprepossessing specimen such as me. "Place Miss Easson on another loom," Thoms ordered at last. "Place her as far as possible from the women who caused the trouble." He hardened his tone. "Carry on, Greer!" he snapped.

"Yes, Mr Thoms." I had never seen Greer as crestfallen as he was while he guided me away.

"I'm still watching you, Easson."

"And I'm watching you, Greer!" I shot back, determined to give as good as I got.

That was the end of the matter, but it was evident to me that my association with Baird had saved me from losing my position. I settled into my new loom, ignored the stares of my work colleagues and wondered what powers the MacGillivray family had. Once again, Baird had saved me from trouble, and my liking for that smiling, open and generous man increased again.

Looking around the dusty, noisy mill in which I seemed destined to spend the remainder of my working life, I thought of Baird's words: "I mean to have you as my wife."

I wish you would, I thought, *oh, I wish you would.* And from where did that tear come, before it slid down my nose, to drip on to my loom? I compared the luxury of Mysore House with this noisy, dusty place and wondered in which world I belonged.

CHAPTER 7

DUNDEE, MAY 1827

Still in a daze of uncertainty over Kenny, I was surprised to see the man himself waiting for me outside the mill. It was seven o'clock on a glorious spring evening, with birds singing above the rumble of wagons over the cobbled roads. Unsure how I felt, or how to act, I decided to walk away from Mr Fairweather.

"Catriona!" Kenny followed, soon catching me. "What's the matter? What's wrong?"

Bending my head, I tried to hurry away, hiding my tears for my feelings were as much in turmoil as they had ever been. Kenny overtook me, for he was always a persistent man.

"Something's bothering you," he said, taking hold of my shoulders. 'Please tell me."

"Get away." I shook him off, lowering my head so Kenny could not see my tears. "I don't want to talk to you."

"What's the matter? It's me, Kenny. What's wrong?" Kenny ran in front of me so I could not get past.

"Get out of my way, please." I stopped dead, keeping my head down as my anger mounted. I did not wish to have an argument in the middle of the street, particularly as Anne and her cronies had gathered to watch, smirking.

"Not until you tell me what is wrong," Kenny insisted, taking hold of my shoulders.

I don't know if our disagreement would have ended with me slapping Kenny, or with him throwing me over his shoulder and stalking away if the coach had not drawn up beside us. Neither Kenny nor I noticed the new arrival. We were so intent on our own affairs until the door opened and Baird jumped out, cane in hand and indignation strong in his face.

"You there!" He shouted, putting a hand on Kenny's arm. "Unhand that woman!"

The words sounded like something from a vulgar novel, but Kenny reacted like any ship's mate under attack. Turning swiftly, he landed a single punch that sent poor Baird spinning against the door of his carriage with his cane flying one way and his hat the other.

"Kenny!" I screamed his name. "What are you doing?"

"Who the devil are you?" Kenny stood over Baird with his fists clenched. "I'd advise you to keep out of my business."

By that time the driver had dismounted and stood at Baird's side, holding a heavy pistol. Baird staggered to his feet with a faint smile on his face; he touched his mouth, from which a trickle of blood dripped on to his chin. I knew that in any physical encounter, Kenny, the ship's mate who dealt with rough men every day of his life, would dispose of the soft-handed Baird in seconds.

"Mr MacGillivray!" Ignoring Kenny and his foul temper, I took my handkerchief and dabbed at the blood on Baird's chin. "Are you all right?"

"Do you know this man?" Kenny did not seem to regret his actions. On the contrary, he seemed ready to continue the conflict with Baird, the coach driver and anybody else who chanced to come along. I heard Anne's delighted laugh in the background and imagined her face as she invented new methods to torment me.

"This is Baird MacGillivray of Mysore House," I said. "He has been very amiable to Mother and me." I looked up from my dabbing operations. "Indeed, he even paid our arrears of rent, or we should be living in the gutter." I thought it best not to mention the Provost's Ball, yet.

"The devil he has," Kenny glanced up as another carriage pulled up at the roadside, and a group of young bucks poured out, shouting as they gathered to watch the fun. "What's to do, Bairdy-boy?" one asked. "Who's this scoundrel?"

"I'll scoundrel you, you blackguard lubbers," Kenny retorted, adding some language that I should not like to repeat in church. I truly do not know why men have to resort to such gutter talk.

The newcomers crowded in, all top hats and fancy weskits, swinging gold-topped canes and talking in affected tones that did nothing to ease the tension. Kenny took a single step back, his fists closed and chin thrust out in defiance.

"Well now, Catriona," Kenny said. "You'd better get away from here. This is no place for a lady."

"A lady!" One of the newcomers jeered. "That guttersnipe thinks the mill-girl is a lady!"

Even before Kenny moved, Baird lifted his cane and slashed at the speaker. "I'll thank you to mind your tongue when speaking of my girl."

"Your girl?" Kenny was still prepared to take on all comers, it seemed. "Your girl? I'll have you know that Miss Easson and I are engaged to be married."

"Oh, is that so?" Baird replaced his hat on his head and faced Kenny, looking him up and down with his smile still in place. "You must be the much-spoken-of Mr Kenneth Fairweather. When I came up, Miss Easson was attempting to walk away, and you were preventing her. I think she is far too good for any tarry-Jack with a ready fist and the manners of a boor."

"Enough!" I had recovered sufficiently for my temper to rise, and I would wager it was hot enough to burn any of these posturing men. "You are acting like children in a school playground," I said severely.

"Punching and insulting each other like little boys! I hope you are all ashamed of yourselves."

"Oh, we are." Baird gave a little bow. "I am ashamed that I ever allowed this nautical fellow sully a lady such as you and I am sure he is ashamed to have lifted his hand to a gentleman."

I coloured at the mocking laughter of Baird's friends. "I think it is time you all went home," I attempted to stand between Kenny and Baird, not sure where my loyalties stood, or my love rested.

"This tarry fellow has struck a gentleman," one of Baird's friends said. "He must make amends for that."

"Mr Fairweather believed he was defending me," I protested, trying desperately to keep the peace. "He was acting for the best possible motive." I faced Kenny. "And Mr MacGillivray believed the same. I am sure Mr Fairweather is prepared to apologise for the blow, and Mr MacGillivray is gracious enough to accept the apology."

"The tarry fellow struck a gentleman," the other man said.

"He did, Oliver," another man added fuel to the fire. "He did. I saw him."

Oliver continued, evidently enjoying the situation as much as Anne, who stood in the background, jeering.

"If the tarry fellow was a gentleman, Baird could challenge him to a duel, or they could fight fist to fist," Oliver said. "But he most evidently is not a gentleman. Take your coachman's whip, Baird, and teach the fellow some manners."

"You will do nothing of the sort," I said. I could imagine Kenny's reaction if Baird or anybody else attempted such a thing.

"Let the lady go." Kenny had not flinched. "She should not be involved in this situation."

I looked around. The crowd was so dense that I could not press free, even if I chose to leave Kenny and Baird to settle their disputes without me.

Baird eyed Kenny up and down, no doubt seeing the hard face of a seaman and the iron muscles and determination of an officer used to giving orders to rough men. "I won't lower myself to a brawl," he said, quite sensibly. "I am not of that class."

I sensed Kenny's anger rising again. "Scared to fight me?"

"No, we will settle this like gentlemen."

"What does that mean?" I demanded.

"A fair competition," Baird said with a gleam in his eyes. "Mr Fairweather is a man of the water, and I am a man of the land, so we will make this equal. We will have one event on land and one at sea."

"I'll fight you anywhere you choose, land or sea or in the air if you can fly," Kenny growled.

"Oh, we won't be fighting." The blood had dried on Baird's chin now, giving him a devil-may-care look that quite suited him. Despite the situation, I could admire the sang-froid with which he took control, for people stepped back when he moved, and even his loud friends treated him with respect. Kenny waited, as unmoving as the Bell Rock Lighthouse. "It's illegal to duel, as you know, and I won't lower myself to fisticuffs like a common rough, however much you might wish to do so. No," Baird shook his elegant head. "We will have a sporting competition with rules." He smiled. "You do understand the notion of rules, I suppose?"

Kenny glanced at me, frowning. "How do you know this jackanapes, Catriona?"

"Listen to me!" Baird cracked his cane against the door of the coach. "I asked, do you understand the notion of rules?"

"I do." If looks could kill, Kenny's glare would have ended the contest there and then.

"Good. Then I propose a riding match on land followed by a rowing race in the river. You can ride a horse, I take it?"

Kenny nodded. "Aye."

"And you must be able to row, being a jack-tar."

"I can row," Kenny agreed.

"Then we shall compete fairly," Baird said. "A point-to-point horse race, followed by a rowing match over a course on the Tay. If we draw, then a foot race followed by a swimming match should be the decider."

"The decider for what?" Kenny's glower did not alter.

"The competition will decide who is the better man," Baird said easily.

"The better man! The better man for what?" Kenny ignored the taunts and jeers of Baird's friends, although I could tell by the manner in which he stood that he was prepared to defend himself if any were so foolish as to attack.

"Oh, did I not make that sufficiently clear for you, my nautical fellow? We are competing for the hand of a lady." Baird bowed in my direction. "The winner of the competition will have the right to woo the most amiable Miss Easson."

I stared at Baird as his friends shouted approval and drummed their hands and canes on the body of their coach, while Anne led her comrades in great hoots of laughter.

"You're a prize, Catty. One of these men will have you for themselves!" Anne gave a high cackle of laughter.

Oh, dear God in heaven, I thought. *However, did it come to such a pass as this?* I raised my voice. "I am not a prize!" I spoke to myself, for Baird and his cronies had filed into their carriages, and the drivers were whipping up.

"I'm not a prize," I said to Kenny, but that worthy was also stalking away with long strides, his fists clenched by his sides.

"I'm not a prize," I whispered to nobody.

CHAPTER 8

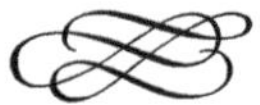

DUNDEE, MAY 1827

"I am not a prize," I said.

I stood outside the front door of Mysore House with Henry the butler standing to straight-faced attention and Baird watching me with quiet amusement.

"You are worth competing for," Baird said.

"I do not wish you to compete for me," I insisted. I had been in confusion since that night outside the mill, wondering what was best to do.

I had tried to discuss things with Mother, but she had only smiled and said: "Imagine having two men fighting over my daughter. You are a lucky woman to inspire such interest."

I did not feel lucky. At that moment, I felt as if I could run away from Dundee and start life anew elsewhere. But I knew I could not. I could not leave Mother alone in her present delicate state of nerves, and nobody would have me anyway, a woman with few skills and no money. I had no choice but to stay where I was and see this foolish business through.

"Imagine having two men prepared to race for you," Mother was sitting at the table, as was her wont. "You should be thrilled."

I was anything but thrilled. As I had fallen out with Kenny over his dealings with Barbara, I refused to speak to him and approached Baird instead. That was why I stood outside Mysore House with Henry the butler watching, poker-faced and Baird smiling obligingly.

"I am not a prize," I repeated.

"You are the best prize a man could ever get," Baird told me, which I decided was more of an insult than a compliment. I refused to be allow myself to be treated as a thing to be won. Baird stepped aside. "Come in, Miss Easson."

I came in, flicking my skirt aside, so it did not touch him. "We must talk," I told him, storming into the drawing room, where Mrs MacGillivray took one look at the expression on my face, raised her eyebrows and drifted away.

"I can see you young people have something to discuss," she said. "These tiffs are better out in the open." She touched my arm lightly and murmured: "I'm glad you have fire, Miss Easson. Don't let him get away with anything. If you give a man an inch, he'll take everything you have." Her smile was strangely comforting, although I thought her gaze lingered a little long on my hips. Had I put on weight in that area recently? I resolved to check in the looking glass as soon as I returned home.

"All right, Miss Easson." Baird gave a brief bow to his mother as he stepped into the room. "Shall we straighten this matter out?"

"Indeed." The anger had been building up inside me, so I was ready to argue with anybody and hang the consequences. I launched myself into an attack. "That was a disgraceful way to act, Mr MacGillivray! I am not going to be a prize in anybody's competition!"

"No, of course not." Baird completely took the wind from my sails with that simple statement, accompanied by his usual smile.

"Oh." I was lost for a reply.

"I came to your place of work and saw a man attack you," Baird explained. "Naturally, I sought to intervene, and the fellow struck me." His bow was even lower and more polite than usual. "I did not know, then, that the man who was preventing you from moving was Mr Fairweather, your intended."

I said nothing, remembering Kenny's liaison with Barbara. Baird seemed less of an ogre than I had thought and his version of the incident tallied with mine.

"If he had not been your intended, I should have horsewhipped him." Baird spoke in a refined, reasonable tone. "As it is, I hope to persuade you that I am the better man in every possible way."

At that moment, I could not argue with Baird's statement. "Perhaps you are," I said.

Baird raised his eyebrows in a manner strikingly reminiscent of his mother. "Well now, Miss Easson, that is very kind of you." He bowed again. "I will endeavour to prove your words true."

At that moment Barbara walked into the room. She stood by the door, looking far more elegant than I ever could, with her perfect poise and classical features, and merely glanced in my direction. I fought down the desire to throw myself at her and scratch out her eyes and gave a polite curtsey instead, hating her.

"Oh. You're here again, Miss Easson," Barbara said flatly and withdrew.

"Yes." I spoke to the closing door. "I'm here." *And Kenneth Fairweather can have you*, I said to myself. "Well, Mr MacGillivray, I do hope you can prove my words correct."

I was pleased to see the surprise on Blair's face. "So do I, Miss Easson." For once, his smile dropped, and there was nothing humorous about the manner in which he examined me. "You are a prize well worth the winning."

Again, I said nothing. I sensed something deep beneath Blair's words; he was more of a man than I had at first thought. But why on earth would a man in his position wish to be with a woman such as me? Why would a gentleman with money and status want to walk out with a mill girl? I discounted the obvious; if that was all he was after, he had neglected a score of opportunities.

"I came here to ask you to withdraw from this contest," I said. "Indeed, Mr MacGillivray, I came to give you a touch of my temper."

Baird smiled at me. "I think that would be an interesting, if perhaps chastening, experience. Do you still have that desire?"

"I might have." I lied, for as Baird's charm wrapped around me, the less I wished to rebuke him.

"I apologise for any distress I caused you," Bard said at once. "That was the opposite of my intention."

I curtseyed. "I know that," I said.

"Then can we still be friends?" Baird's eyes were laughing as he bowed.

"Yes," I decided firmly. "We can still be friends. But I am no prize," I warned.

"No," Baird said. "You are far better than a prize, but if I have to compete for you, then I shall compete to win." He nodded. "You may kiss goodbye to Mr Kenneth Fairweather."

"Mr Fairweather will not be an easy man to overcome," I warned, "particularly at sea."

"I am glad to hear you say that," Baird said. "I should not care to think of a lady such as you falling for a poor specimen of a man."

Even as I smiled, I felt apprehensive. Much as I hated the thought of Kenny with Barbara and resented their being together, I did not wish him to lose badly. I hoped that he would give a good account of himself. Even more, I hoped that he would fall out with Barbara and return his affection to me. I looked at Baird and all that he represented. I thought he was a good man, but I did not love him.

I still loved Kenny Fairweather, damn him for a double-dealing blackguard.

Dundee Law is undoubtedly the most exceptional viewpoint in the vicinity of Dundee. It stands more than 500 feet high, a grassy hill surmounted by an ancient hill fort or Roman fort or Druidical ruins or something of the sort. I really don't know what it is, but it's old, and it's there. The views are tremendous, from the Sidlaw Hills to the north to the green fields of Fife to the south and eastward along the silver-blue Firth of Tay to the German Ocean.

However, on that Sunday morning, nobody was admiring the view. We were all intent on the forthcoming race. The dawn rose, silver-pink from the Tay, ghosting across the huddled mud-grey town below, where the smoke spiralled from hundreds of chimneys, and the barking of a dog rose upwards. We gathered on the sheep-cropped summit of the Law, a score of men in tall hats, a dozen horses and three women, including the obnoxious Barbara and me. I noticed that Barbara ignored me as studiously as I avoided her, although I experienced a great desire to run up and push her down the Law.

"Rules." Oliver had appointed himself as spokesperson of the meeting. He stood in an outrageously bright blue coat above cripplingly tight trousers and a weskit of the most distressing yellow. "We have two contestants for the hand of the amiable Miss Catriona Easson."

There was a small ripple of applause, a huzza or two and quizzical looks in my direction. I looked away, not wishing to be the centre of attention, although Barbara glanced at me and away again. I wondered if she was supporting her brother or my betrothed. I took a deep breath of the crisp air, wondering whom I wished to win. Should I support Baird, who had been so kind to my mother and me? Or should I shout for Kenny, my intended, but who I had seen so close to Barbara?

Oliver lifted a hand to silence the buzz. "On my left, may I have the pleasure of introducing Mr Baird MacGillivray of Mysore House?"

Baird leapt lightly on to the back of his horse, a pure-black Arab with a white splash on his chest, and lifted a hand to encourage the crowd's cheers. Dressed in white breeches and a light-grey linen shirt, he was bare-headed with his hair unfashionably long, and looked athletic and thoroughly at home in the saddle.

"Zeus and I will win the day." He patted the neck of his horse, smiled to me, then gazed forward, marking out the course.

"On my right," Oliver continued, "we have Mr Kenneth Fairweather of the brig *Admiral Duncan*."

I watched Kenny mount his horse, a brown-and-white gelding I had never seen before. I was about to cross to him but I stopped when Barbara stepped forward and held the horse's bridle. The two looked very comfortable together.

I felt the pain like a knife twisting inside me. *Kenny! How can you do this to me?*

Oliver was talking again, with some of the crowd keeping quiet to hear his words of wisdom.

"The race is a point to point between the Law and the observatory on Kinpurnie Hill and back." He pointed vaguely in the direction of Kinpurnie, one of the Sidlaw Hills, half-visible in the morning gloom, where the tower of the old observatory thrust out like a stone thumb. I stood back. I had no idea how good a rider Kenny was, but I could see that Baird sat securely, as would be expected of somebody with his background. Kenneth was a seaman, not a horseman.

"I've never seen a horse race before," I confided to Mrs MacGillivray who had appeared at my side, leading her horse by the reins but still as tall and elegant as if she had been in her own drawing room.

"It's a point-to-point," Mrs MacGillivray reminded me kindly. "That means they will ride as fast as they can between the two points, jumping fences or walls, crossing any burns and riding up hills."

I nodded, unsure if Kenny's riding skills were up to the challenge. "Mr MacGillivray seems comfortable in the saddle."

"It's a good seat that makes all the difference," Mrs MacGillivray explained. 'Look at Baird now, he sits quietly, with his legs still and his shoulders, hips and heels all aligned, yet he looks strong in the saddle.'

I nodded. "Your son looks like a centaur," I said, "as if he was born to the saddle." Yet, even as I spoke, I had one eye on Kenny, who was leaning forward, talking to Barbara.

Before Mrs MacGillivray could reply, Oliver raised his hand again. "Keep clear of the riders!" he ordered.

"Wait!" Ignoring Oliver's command, I hurried across to Kenny and Baird. Barbara promptly dropped Kenny's reins and stalked away with her back erect. "Have you two not seen sense yet?" I demanded. "You cannot go through with this silliness."

"Stand aside, Catriona, if you please." With his nautical cap on his head and his unsteady seat in the saddle, Kenny looked as ill-prepared as I had ever seen him. "We have a race to run."

"Your friend is correct, Miss Easson," Baird said. "When the gun goes off, there will be such a turmoil that the horses will trample you underfoot. You should stand clear for your own safety."

"Ready!" Oliver called, raising a pistol in the air. "I will count to three!"

"Best stand clear, Catriona."

I tried to think there was a genuine concern in Kenny's face until I saw Barbara smiling at him. I stepped out of the road and further away from Barbara as Oliver cocked his pistol, with the click sounding slightly sinister on that windy hillside. The crowd grew silent, with only the barking of that stupid dog and my irregular breathing disturbing the peace. Barbara lifted a single finger in Kenny's direction.

Oliver waited, heightening the tension. "One, two, three!"

The sound of the pistol was like the knell of doom. White smoke spurted from the barrel and the riders were away.

In little more time than it took to blink, Baird had thrust in his spurs, cracked his riding crop across the rump of Zeus and was slithering and sliding down the steep slope of the Law. After a glance at me, Kenny followed, with less skill and urgency, so by the time he was halfway down the hill, Baird was well ahead. I could hear Kenny shouting to encourage his horse.

"Come on, Jane. Come on, my beauty!"

Jane. Even the horse's name seemed uninspiring compared to Baird's Zeus, the king of the Greek Gods. *Poor Kenny*, I thought, *you don't stand a chance.*

I watched them until they were out of sight at the foot of the hill, and had an occasional glimpse of them in the low country between the Law and Kinpurnie Hill, and then wondered what to do. There was no point in trying to follow on foot, so I could only fret and hope they came back fairly quickly. After 10 minutes, I could no longer see them as they vanished into the morning mist.

Oliver was perched on somebody's shoulders, peering through a telescope as he gave a disjointed commentary. "I can see Kinpurnie Observatory," he said. "I've posted Peter and Nigel there. Peter will ensure they both touch the stonework and Nigel will signal to me when both are on their way back. When the first rider reaches the observatory, I will raise my hand, like so!" Oliver demonstrated for the benefit of those people who had never seen a hand before. "When the second rider reaches the observatory, I will raise my other hand." He did so and then continued gazing through the telescope.

I waited, aware that, every so often, heads would turn toward me as the ostensible cause of this race. The men were grinning, while the women looked critical as they viewed my appearance and wondered why two men would wish to compete in such a breakneck manner for somebody as ordinary as me. I closed my mouth firmly, wondering what I would say if the obnoxious Barbara spoke to me.

"How does it feel, being important?" Mrs MacGillivray had handed her horse to a servant and approached me. She ignored a spatter of cold rain.

"I don't feel important," I said. "I think all of this is rather silly and a trifle embarrassing."

Mrs MacGillivray gave a rueful smile. "Men are rather silly things, Miss Easson. You'll find that they don't get any less silly as they get older. Worse, if anything, for they lack the excuse of youth. I find that the best thing to do is to allow them their silliness and be prepared to patch up what they break."

I managed to smile at her words. "I'll try to remember that."

"They'll be approaching Kinpurnie Hill now," Mrs MacGillivray said. "Tell me, do you object if I call you Catriona?"

"No, not at all," I responded. When one is the prize for two silly men racing horses across half of Scotland, it did not seem to matter what term of address an older woman used.

"Good. I feel as if you are family already."

I said nothing to that. I still was not sure who I hoped to win. I peered into the slowly clearing mist, hoping for a glimpse of Baird and Zeus, or Kenny and Jane. I saw neither.

"Tell me, Catriona," Mrs MacGillivray said, "who do you want to win, in your heart of hearts?"

If I were a diplomatic woman, I would have replied Baird of course. As it was, I hesitated, thinking of the years I had known Kenny as well as his betrayal with Barbara. "In my heart of hearts," I said bitterly, "I wish this foolishness had never started." I could sense Mrs MacGillivray's disapproval.

"You must prefer Baird to that sailor." Mrs MacGillivray's voice was like Arctic ice.

At that moment, I caught sight of Barbara, and I preferred Baird's *horse* to that sailor, let alone Baird. "Yes," I said, with an emphatic nod. "Baird is a gentleman of generosity and breeding. I don't believe he would ever break his word to a woman."

Mrs MacGillivray's chilling disapproval melted as the sun rose above the Tay. "He has some good points," she allowed. "Look!"

Oliver lifted one hand in the air, a signal that one of the riders had reached Kinpurnie Hill and had begun the return journey. I did not know which rider but guessed that Baird was the faster of the two. Although I was sick at heart with Kenny's betrayal, some small part of me still wished that he would at least give a good account of himself. I may still have loved him, then. I am not sure.

I waited for Oliver to lift his second hand but it remained by his side. What had happened to Kenny?

"Do you have many brothers and sisters, Catriona?" Mrs

MacGillivray was eyeing me again, with a strange curiosity in her expression.

"I have three sisters," I said.

Mrs MacGillivray seemed delighted at this intelligence. "I had not heard that. Where are they all now? I know they are not living in your present address." She smiled as if at some secret joke that we were supposed to share, yet I did not.

"All my sisters are younger than me and married." I looked away. "I am the last of the family."

"How strange," Mrs MacGillivray said. "And you are such an amiable, well-set-up woman with a lot to offer." She looked away momentarily. "I am astonished that a man has not snapped you up, Catherine."

"It's Catriona," I corrected.

"Yes, of course. Would you like children, Catriona?"

"I would indeed. I'd like any amount of children."

Mrs MacGillivray's smile was as broad as anything her son could muster. I thought she was going to embrace me, but instead, she patted my arm. "That is as it should be."

At that point, Oliver lifted his left arm. It had taken the second rider that length of time to reach Kinpurnie Hill and begin the return journey.

"Baird will be here soon," Mrs MacGillivray said with satisfaction. "And that will be the first victory to him." She turned to me with another smile. "He learned to ride before he could walk, you know, and played polo and rode at tent-pegging in India when he was just seven years old."

Poor Kenny, I thought, a sailor on horseback is always an ungainly thing, and this foolish wager set him against an expert. At least he would have the advantage in the second stage. Kenny was as much at home at sea as Baird was on the back of a horse. From the corner of my eye, I watched Barbara, wondering what she was thinking, wondering if I could approach her and ask what her intentions were with Kenny.

She could retaliate by asking me what my intentions were with Baird. It was only then that I realised I was the pot calling the kettle black. I felt as if somebody had drawn a veil from my eyes. How stupid I was! I was every bit as bad as Kenny.

We had to wait only a few moments before Baird arrived, riding with almost casual arrogance, although Zeus was flecked with foam and sweating from the ride. Baird dismounted with a flourish, waved to his sister and strode towards me.

"Well, Miss Easson, that was easy enough. The better man won and is halfway to securing your affection."

"Miss Easson says we may call her Catriona," Mrs MacGillivray said. "Well done on your victory, Baird, but I expected nothing else."

Baird bowed. "Thank you, Mother. Your sailor fellow took a tumble, I fear, Miss Easson."

"Is he hurt?" I asked, perhaps too quickly for a woman who had been betrayed.

"You will see when he eventually appears," Baird said casually. "Now, I must see to Zeus." Although sweat had dampened his clothes and beaded his forehead, Baird's breathed as calmly as if he had merely walked down his garden path.

"I think the victor deserves a kiss," Mrs MacGillivray suggested with an arch smile.

"I am still betrothed to Mr Fairweather," I reminded. "The contest is only half done."

Baird, to give him credit, accepted my words. "You are an honourable woman," he said. "A real lady, in fact."

Mrs MacGillivray exchanged glances with Baird. "Mr Fairweather does not deserve a woman such as you," she said.

Again, at that moment, I agreed. Men who abuse the trust of their betrothed do not deserve any consideration. But I thought I still loved him. Despite his behaviour, I still harboured feelings for Kenny and now wondered if I had also acted improperly.

"Catriona was telling me that she had a numerous family," Mrs MacGillivray told Baird.

"Oh, indeed?" Baird graced me with another of his bright smiles. "Catriona has many sisters, and all still alive, I believe."

"Not quite," I corrected. "Mother lost two children when they were young."

Mrs MacGillivray nodded. "Such things do happen," she said. "Your mother is to be praised for keeping so many alive."

I did not reply to that. I knew that the loss of two children still weighed heavily on Mother. She would not accept any praise for being a mother, and she would not give any praise. It was not her way.

"Oh, look. I believe Mr Fairweather is coming at last," Mrs MacGillivray said.

The crowd had grown somewhat since the race's beginning, so there must have been a couple of hundred people gathered on the bald summit of the Law. Ignoring my manners, I pushed to the front to see Kenny arrive. Both Kenny and his horse looked fully blown as they climbed the hill, with Kenny drooping in the saddle and Jane covered in foam. As Baird had said, Kenny had taken a tumble somewhere and mud covered his left side from ankle to brow. He had lost his cap somewhere along the route and cut a sorry figure, compared to the nonchalant elegance of Baird. I felt rather sorry for him, indeed, and possibly a little ashamed that my intended had done so badly. However, I did clap as he staggered to the summit.

"Well done, Kenny." Ignoring the stares and comments of the crowd, I walked forward to take hold of Jane's bridle. "You fell, I see."

"Yes," Kenny said shortly. "I also lost."

"Mr MacGillivray is something of an expert rider." I tried to soothe the pain of defeat. "It is no disgrace to lose to him."

"And how would you know that?" Kenny slid to the ground, looking muddy and bedraggled.

"Mrs MacGillivray informed me that her son had ridden since early childhood."

"Did she?" Kenny muttered, attempting to clean some of the mud from his person, but succeeding only in smearing it the more.

"You'd best go and clean yourself up," I said. "You are quite a sight. I hope you did not injure yourself when you tumbled."

"No," Kenny said, although I saw him favour his left wrist.

As it was apparent that Kenny was not in the mood to talk, I stepped back into the crowd.

"Kenneth." Barbara must have waited until I withdrew before she pushed forward. Looking as graceful as ever, she stepped toward Kenny, putting her delicate hand on his arm. I felt my anger bubble inside me, nearly removing my capacity for rational thought. *How dare that woman touch Kenny?*

No. I must control my anger. I turned away, calling the brazen Barbara various names under my breath. She was a hussy, a minx, a scoundrel. Those names and others too foul to repeat scrambled through my head as I walked away with my emotions in turmoil.

By that time, the morning was well advanced, full daylight lit the Law, and the melody of a dozen bells was summoning the godly to church. The crowd began to disperse, men helping women on to the rough track back to Dundee or mounting horses for the descent. Dogs and children gambolled, a thimble-rigger tried to gather a crowd and a policeman in his long coat and stovepipe hat placed a heavy hand on the shoulder of a pickpocket. All life was on the Law that morning, with my drama only one of many.

"Where are you going, Catriona?" Baird appeared at my side, his voice gentle.

"Back home," I spoke more shortly than I had intended.

"Are you going to church this morning?"

"I am," I said. "Mother and I always worship on the Sabbath."

Baird kept pace with me, step for step, with men and women making space, as they always did for Baird.

"Is Zeus all right without you?" I asked, still snappily.

"The servants will take him back to the stables," Baird said. "I prefer your company to that of a horse."

I could not help my reply. "Others seem to prefer the company of your sister."

"Oh?" Glancing over his shoulder, Baird nodded. "Oh, Fairweather. I see what you mean. They do appear rather cosy together, don't they?"

"Rather." I lengthened my stride, not wishing to talk.

"Barbara will speak to anybody," Baird said carelessly. "You are angered?" He was sufficiently perceptive to see my dark frown and the set of my shoulders.

"I am angered," I said.

Baird remained at my side, still keeping level as I strode down the hill. "Would you like me to accompany you home?"

"I wish to be alone at present." I was far too curt with a man who desired only to be friendly.

"Then I shall leave you to your thoughts," Baird responded, stepping back at once. "Will you be at the boat race?"

"I shall," I said without looking back. "And I hope that you win that handsomely.'

When anger takes over my mouth, I say things that I later regret. When I spoke those words, I fully meant them. My mind was in such turmoil that I did not consider what I was saying.

CHAPTER 9

DUNDEE, MAY 1827

Mother and I attended St Mary's, right in the heart of the city and only a five-minute walk from Milne's Close. It was a church full of comforting memories, for Mother had married here, and all her children, including me, had been christened at the font. That morning, Mother was rather quiet. She sang the psalms in a small voice and closed her eyes tightly during prayers, as if trying to prove her religious fervour by the firmness of her eyelids, rather like young children trying to convince their parents they were sleeping in bed.

I watched her, worrying about the state of her nerves, and guided her to the church door when the minister gave his final blessing.

"How are you, Mrs Easson?" The Reverend Grieve always said farewell to his congregation as they came out through the stone arch.

"I am very well, thank you, minister." Mother produced a bright smile that was as false as any mountebank on stage.

"I am glad to hear it," Mr Grieve replied solemnly. "I know you have been having some bad times recently."

Mother nodded. "Thank you, minister. You lost your wife as well."

Mr Grieve bowed. "My Mary has been with the Lord 14 months today."

"She was a good woman," Mother said.

The minister nodded grave-faced. "And you, Miss Easson," he turned to me. "I hope you are looking after your mother."

"As best I can," I assured him.

"I have heard some disturbing things about you." The minister's gaze did not stray from my eyes. "About you going to the Provost's Ball and riding in coaches with a man who is not your intended. A Mr Baird MacGillivray, I believe."

There are few secrets in a small town such as Dundee. "That is true," I said. "I helped Mr Baird MacGillivray when his coach was in difficulty and, in return, he invited me to the Provost's Ball." I did not mention the contests or the intended prize.

The minister nodded, his eyes probing. "I don't know this Mr MacGillivray – he is not in my parish," he said. "I must call on him."

"He is at Mysore House." Mother was eager to share her knowledge. "Mr Baird MacGillivray is a gentleman of the finest honour and integrity."

Mr Grieve nodded again. He was a tall man in his late middle age whom I had always found decent and genuinely caring for his flock. "I do not doubt your words, Mrs Easson. However, I think it better if Miss Easson restricted her attentions to Mr Kenneth Fairweather."

I accepted the criticism. I knew the minister was giving what he thought was good advice in my best interests. I have never been angered by people who are genuinely trying to help, however misguided they may be.

"I will come around tonight, Mrs Easson," the minister said. "There is no need to prepare anything." He lowered his voice. "Between you and me, Mrs Easson, by the time I have done my rounds of the parish, I have more tea splashing around inside me than there is water in the ocean."

Mother gave a small, welcome smile. "We will look forward to your visit, Mr Grieve."

The minister gave me a significant look. "Perhaps Miss Easson should visit Mr Fairweather and ensure he does not misunderstand her meeting with Mr MacGillivray."

"I'll see Kenny Fairweather tonight," I promised.

"Good." Mr Grieve gave a small nod of approval.

That decision pleased me, for the boat race was scheduled for that evening, and I had no wish to leave mother alone.

Evenings on the Firth of Tay can be dull and dismal, with the smoke from Dundee's factory chimneys hanging heavy on the water and the hush of the river slightly sinister. That Sunday evening was the opposite. At nine o'clock, the sun was dipping to the west, sending slivers of glorious orange along the river, highlighting the silvery ripples that broke among the dozing seals on the sandbanks and reflecting from the windows of the houses along the river bank.

"Well then," Oliver began. He was clearly acting as master of ceremonies again.

We stood beside the Craig Pier with the Fifie ferries moored for the night. Quite a crowd had gathered and a host of seagulls were circling above. Baird stood within a circle of his admirers, laughing as he stretched his muscles, while Kenny stood alone. Two small skiffs waited for the contestants. Both were without masts but supplied with a pair of oars. Although they were similar in size and design, with a pointed bow and flat stern, the closest was undoubtedly the most elaborately painted boat I had ever seen, purple and blue with two eyes in the bow. Her name, *Nabob of Mysore*, was picked out in gold leaf across the stern. I did not need to ask who owned that vessel. The second was a drab brown, with plain *Jane* across the stern in simple black letters.

I remembered, belatedly, that Kenny's mother was named Jane. Kenny was remaining as true to the Fairweather family as Baird was to the MacGillivrays.

"How are you, Kenny?" I kept my voice neutral to show my continued displeasure. "Do you have any ill-effects from this morning's misadventure?"

"None." Kenny looked hale and hearty, despite a bruise across the side of his head, although I thought he was still favouring his left arm.

"Are you ready to even the score?"

"Yes."

Honestly, it was hard work trying to squeeze a conversation from that man. I don't know why I bothered. I should have given up long before I did.

"You'll be better on the water. It's your element."

"Yes."

I wondered what I had to do to get more than a monosyllable from Kenny. "I doubt that Mr MacGillivray will have your experience of boats."

"No."

"We're here to cheer you on, Mr Fairweather!" I was relieved when a gang of men from *Admiral Duncan* rolled along the pier. Weathered in appearance, they walked with a nautical swagger and spoke in a language that only old salts could understand as they ignored Baird's more refined crew.

"Is this your gal?" The Duncans crowded around me, nutmeg-brown of face, chewing tobacco as their bare feet slapped the ground.

"Yes." Kenny was as laconic with his shipmates as he was with me, which was something, I suppose.

"She's not bad." One stocky, bearded man gave his considered opinion. He fingered his gold earring. "Who's the opposition?"

"Him." Kenny nodded to Baird, who was watching the arrival of the Duncans with undisguised amusement.

"He looks like a right gentleman." The bearded man managed to make the term "gentleman" sound like an insult. When others of Kenny's crew added what they thought of Baird I decided it was time for me to withdraw before my ears bled from the salty language.

"I'll leave you to make ready," I said.

The Duncans gave me a rousing send-off, with cheers and nautical expressions that I was glad I did not understand. Sometimes ignorance can be a blessing when mixing with Dundee seamen.

"Are you excited?" I did not see from where Mrs MacGillivray appeared. She wore a sensible long cloak against the evening air and tapped a riding whip against her leg. "I should be excited if two men were racing for my hand."

"I am still not sure that I wish to be a prize in a big boys' game."

"There are worse things to be," Mrs MacGillivray said. "At least Baird and that Fairweather fellow are actively working to gain you." When she looked at me, her smile was crooked. "I was won in a game of cards."

I started at this admission. "My God," I blasphemed, which was a sin on any day of the week, let alone on the Sabbath. "Who was playing?"

"Mr MacGillivray was one of the players," Mrs MacGillivray said. "I can't remember some of the others, but they included an officer or two of John Company and an Indian rajah." Her smile widened. "I could have been a rani if the rajah won, with hundreds of servants and thousands of square miles of land."

I blinked, not fully understanding. "A rani?"

"The Indian equivalent of a queen," Mrs MacGillivray explained calmly as if every Dundee wife found her husband on the turn of a card. She smiled. "It's quite a thought, isn't it? Mr MacGillivray won me on the last cards. It was the queen of hearts, as I recall." Her smile was a little wistful, I thought. "Now you are the prize, and two strong young men are competing for you." She gave a throaty chuckle. 'I envy you, Catriona. Whoever wins, you win, although Baird has a lot more to offer than Mr Fairweather."

I gave a little shiver of disquiet. It seemed as if Mrs MacGillivray counted material possessions as the most important thing a man could offer. Many women did, of course. In a way, all marriage was a gamble, with men seeking one thing, women another. Men often seemed to want only an agreeable partner in bed while women were searching for security, and love was seen as less important than a pretty face or a fat bank balance.

Now you're being cynical, I told myself sternly. *Neither Kenny nor Baird thinks like that.*

Standing on the keel of an upturned boat on the jetty, Oliver loaded and raised a pistol. The crack of the shot shocked half the crowd so that some of the women screamed and one elderly man put a hand on his heart. A score of seagulls lifted into the air, screaming.

"Ladies, gentlemen and those who do not deserve either title." Oliver could give Orator Hunt a run for his money, I thought. "We are gathered here to witness the second round in a fascinating contest between two men hoping to win the hand of a fair lady."

Some of the crowd gave a loud huzza and waved their hats in the air. Others whistled, while Baird's supporters began to chant his name. The crew of *Admiral Duncan* were silent for a few moments and then broke into a roar of, "Come on Kenneth! Come on, Kenneth!" that drowned out most of the rest. Whatever else, Kenny had plenty of support on this leg of the contest. As faces turned toward me as the cause of the excitement, I kept my expression neutral. I had no desire to be seen grinning like a mountebank as men competed for my affections.

Oliver watched for a while as he reloaded his pistol, and then fired it in the air again, creating instant silence. "The two contestants will row out to Tayport High Lighthouse and back."

Most of the crowd stared towards the south coast of the Firth to see the lighthouse that thrust upwards from Tayport harbour entrance; a few continued to scrutinise me as if I were a piece of meat on display in a flesher's shop window. I looked at Kenny, and then at Baird, and back to Kenny again.

Oliver spoke once more. "Those of you who were present at this morning's race will remember that I posted a man on Kinpurnie Hill to mark the arrival of each contestant. This time I have stationed a man at the lighthouse to ensure they keep to the rules and signal to me when they are homeward bound."

Again the crowd cheered, yelled, whistled or chanted, depending on their desires. I took a deep breath and abruptly exhaled when I saw the beauteous Barbara once more, standing close to Kenny. She said something, touched his arm and stepped back as he swung down into his skiff.

"Damn you," I said, rolling the words around my mouth in perverse enjoyment. I was not prone to swearing so I felt slightly shocked that there was no immediate crash of thunder and blast of lightning to eradicate me for cursing on the Sabbath. Still, perhaps the good Lord made allowances for my state of nervous agitation. He is a caring Father, after all.

Kenny and Baird sat in their respective boats, holding the oars and waiting for the gunshot that was to be the signal to start the race. Kenny's crewmen were chanting his name in a continuous roar, with their words enhanced by a great cloud of tobacco smoke that drifted along the pier. Baird's cronies were taller and more elegant, but not as skilled in shouting. Perhaps they had never had to roar orders over a German Ocean gale. In between these groups of men, splashes of bright colour showed where women stood to watch the fun, with a sprinkling of children and dogs animating the scene with their antics. Looking for Barbara, I saw her staring intently at the two men, her gaze shifting from one to the other as if uncertain who to support, her brother or the seaman whom she seemed determined to pluck from my side.

Well, I thought, *well, Madam Barbara of the classical beauty, you may have him and welcome, and I hope he treats you with as much loyalty as he does me, the double-dealing sea-dog.* I had entirely forgotten my own double standards in my anger at Barbara.

Raising his pistol once more, Oliver fired, to the now-familiar chorus of screams and cheers. I was not surprised when Kenny pulled ahead at once, throwing himself at the oars as if they were mortal enemies rather than shaped lengths of polished wood. Standing on the pier, I watched in silence, unsure for whom to cheer, unsure whom I wished to win. The crew of *Admiral Duncan* had no such doubts and roared their lungs out, waving their hats in the air to encourage their man. The sun was dipping, sending orange shafts across the Tay, gleaming on the fields of Fife, giving a nearly sublime beauty to the scene.

I watched as the skiffs raced across the Firth, with Kenny increasing his lead with every stroke. Eventually, the growing dim meant I could no longer distinguish the contestants. Standing on his boat's hull, Oliver was watching through his telescope, giving a running commentary on the progress of the race.

"Fairweather is increasing his lead, with MacGillivray working hard to catch up. Now they are halfway across the Tay, with Fairweather at least a hundred yards ahead. There's a collier mid-channel, and both boats are pulling to avoid her with Fairweather's lead increasing all the time."

I looked away, to see Barbara watching me through thoughtful eyes. I wondered if I should approach her and ask what her intentions were with Kenny. If I did, she could retaliate by asking what mine were with Baird. I swore again, finding comfort in the foul words. I had never before understood why men used such vile language, but now I began to. These words allow one to give vent to emotions that could otherwise corrode inside one and give rise to bitterness. Having thus justified myself, I swore again, happily this time, although ensuring that nobody else heard my foul-mouthed tirade. Barbara could wait until I had formulated a plan to deal appropriately with her.

"Fairweather has reached the lighthouse," Oliver reported. I had nearly forgotten about the race in my preoccupation with language and the despicable Barbara. "MacGillivray is far behind. Fairweather has turned and is on the homeward leg."

From my stance, both skiffs appeared little more than dots on the darkening Firth, while the sails of the collier vessel gleamed in the dying rays of the sun. I had to depend on Oliver's words to be assured who was in the lead.

"There they go," Oliver said. 'Fairweather is a quarter of the way back across the Firth, and MacGillivray has only reached the lighthouse. It appears as if Fairweather will be the victor with time to spare."

I looked for Barbara. She was standing beside Baird's friends, staring over the river. As I watched, one of the elegants spoke to her, and she slipped the calfskin glove off her left hand. I felt a stab of intense jealousy as the sun flashed from a ring on her hand. That must have been what Kenny gave her outside Mysore House; she was displaying her proof of engagement to Kenny, flaunting his ring when she must surely know that Kenny had never given me even the slightest token of his affection.

"Fairweather is increasing his lead," Oliver continued. "No; he has stopped! He's lost an oar!"

"What?" I looked up. "Kenny's lost an oar?"

The crew of *Admiral Duncan* roared their disbelief. "Our Kenny wouldnae dae that!" They added expletives that would make one's hair curl.

"He has!" Oliver continued. "Fairweather is floundering. He's holding one oar. MacGillivray is closing the gap!"

I caught Barbara's eye as she put her hands over her mouth and then looked towards me. I thought she tried to smile until the expression on my face warned her off, for, at that moment, my thoughts were anything but ladylike. *You've got something to do with that oar,* I thought. *You want Kenny to lose so he'll be all yours.*

"MacGillivray is catching up." Oliver continued his commentary.

Having suddenly lost interest in Mr Kenneth Fairweather and his amorous antics with that other woman, I deliberately ignored the boat race. I would have turned and walked away had the crowd not been so dense, so instead fixed my gaze on Barbara who seemed intent on flashing her ring to everybody who was in the vicinity. She was laughing with Baird's friends and clapping as her brother overtook Kenneth and headed for the pier.

No more divided loyalties, my girl, I thought.

"MacGillivray has taken the lead," Oliver continued, although by that time we could all see he was nearing the pier, rowing as if his life depended on it, throwing himself back with each pull. Behind him, Kenneth had resorted to sculling his boat with his single oar and, despite all his efforts, seemed to be standing still in comparison to Baird. I could not help but watch, feeling Kenny's frustration even from the shore.

"We have a victor," Oliver announced as Baird pulled up alongside the pier and leapt ashore to the cheers of his friends and loud hooting from the crew of *Admiral Duncan*. "Where is his prize?"

"Here she is!" Somebody pointed to me. Within seconds, half the crowd seemed to be pushing me towards Baird. His grin was as wide as ever, and I could see the breadth of his chest as he laboured for breath. I also saw a hint of curly-crisp chest hair peeping from his shirt where a button was missing. *He needs a wife to look after him,* I thought absently.

"I have won you fair and square," Baird said. "Now I claim at least a kiss."

I felt my heart beat faster. While one part of me was not loath to kiss this eminently kissable man, another held on to the faint hope that I was mistaken about Kenny and that he was still faithful to me.

"I did not agree to that, Mr MacGillivray," I said.

"Oh, kiss the fellow," somebody shouted. Some of the rougher elements of the crowd joined in, chanting: "Kiss him, kiss him," at the top of their beery voices. "Go on, lass; he won you as his prize!"

"No," I disagreed. "I am not a prize to be won in a silly boys' game."

"No?" Baird said in pretended astonishment, reached forward, grabbed me in both hands, pulled me close and planted a kiss precisely in the centre of my forehead. When the crowd cheered, I struggled to get away.

"Kiss her, kiss her," the crowd chanted, and Mrs MacGillivray laughed.

"Oh, for goodness' sake, Baird, give her a real kiss or don't kiss her at all."

"No!" My protest was in vain as Baird pulled me close again. Although he held me tight, his kiss was surprisingly gentle, with his salty lips against mine. If the situation had been different, I might have enjoyed that kiss, but in front of a cheering crowd, I felt only embarrassment.

When Baird eventually released me, I was scarlet with shame. Pushing him away, I said, "Oh," or something equally unhelpful.

The crowd parted before me, some laughing, some looking sympathetic, others merely staring as I ran towards Kenny with most of my anger lost in my desire to console him. When I reached the end of the pier, I saw Kenny landing with his single-sculled boat. He stared at me for a moment and turned away, either in shame at losing or because he had transferred his affections to Barbara.

"Kenny?" I said his name aloud, but he did not look although I was sure he had heard me. I stood there, in the middle of a crowd of some hundreds, feeling as alone as I had ever been in my life. All these people must have witnessed Kenny rejecting me. Lifting my skirt above my ankles, I pushed through the mob and ran home, trying to hide my still blazing face. How had Kenny managed to lose an oar? He was a seaman; he had worked on seagoing vessels since he was 10 years old, and on small boats since he first drew breath. I had never known him even catch a crab before, let alone drop an oar. I knew the answer, of course. It had been deliberate. Kenny had lost on purpose because he was no longer interested in me.

"Catriona!" I heard Baird's voice as I passed him. Shaking my head, I ran on. There would be plenty of time to speak to Baird later. In the meantime, I had nothing to say, and nothing could fill the void in my heart.

CHAPTER 10

DUNDEE, MAY 1827

With my last hope for Kenny extinguished, I ran through Dundee's streets until sense overtook my passion. What was I upset over? Two silly men agreed to a contest; nobody ever asked if I agreed to be a prize. Well, then, let them make fools of themselves for I wanted no part in it. Kenny evidently preferred the beautiful Barbara to me, while Baird? I struggled to find something negative to think about Baird, except for his proposing the contest. That was surely enough, I told myself angrily, and then remembered how he had paid our arrears of rent.

Washing my face at a public well, I slowed down to compose myself before arriving home. I had no desire to further upset Mother's nerves by appearing unhappy. Taking a deep breath, I composed myself, squared my shoulders and walked up the close to our house.

"Catriona!" Mother was at her customary place at the table. "How was the race?"

"It was interesting," I said, acutely aware of the minister's presence opposite mother. I had forgotten Reverend Grieve would be in the house. "Although it was hardly the right thing to do on the Sabbath."

"Well said," the minister said approvingly. "Your mother has been telling me about your misadventures, Miss Easson."

Unsure what else to do, I bobbed in a curtsey to him. I find that a curtsey is a useful device in most situations. It allows me a few moments to think of an appropriate response and allows everybody else to believe that I am respectful and polite.

"It has been an interesting few days, Minister."

"My name is Mr Grieve," the minister said, "or Reverend Grieve if you prefer." He had stood up when I entered, so I motioned him to sit down again.

"Who won the race?" Mother asked.

"Mr Baird MacGillivray," I said. "Mr Fairweather lost an oar."

"He lost an oar? Kenneth Fairweather lost an oar?" Mother was astonished. "How on earth did he manage to lose an oar?"

"I wondered that myself." I did not wish to voice my suspicions in case I further damaged Mother's nerves.

"The Lord works in mysterious ways to show his disapproval of people's actions on the Sabbath," Mr Grieve said.

When Mother smiled, I was surprised at such a rare occurrence.

"You are right, Mr Grieve. It must have been the Lord's work." Mother said. "He is telling you something, Catriona."

"What is He telling me?"

"Perhaps he is guiding you towards a better choice of man," Mother said. "You don't wish to be married to a seagoing man."

"Why not, pray?" Mr Grieve asked. "I believe that you and Mr Kenneth Fairweather have had an arrangement for some time."

I had to bite my tongue then, for fear of saying too much and upsetting Mother. "There is an arrangement."

"I have always found Mr Fairweather to be the most honest of men and a member of a God-fearing and decent family," Mr Grieve said. "I believe he would be the best of husbands in that respect." He gave a small smile. "Perhaps he is not as loquacious as some."

"He is as close-mouthed as a rock." I could have said a lot worse.

"Would you prefer him to be as chattering as a Frenchman?" Mr Grieve asked, with a smile in his eyes. "You might be glad of a quiet husband, Catriona. Does he drink?"

I shook my head. "I have never seen him the worse for drink."

"Is he violent?"

"I have only seen him violent once." I forced myself to agree Kenny's good points.

"Oh, when was that, pray?" Mr Grieve asked.

I explained about the incident outside the mill. Mr Grieve listened, nodding. "I see. He did not precipitate the violence but acted in what he believed was defence of you, his intended. Perhaps we can forgive him his actions for even Christ lost his temper to defend his family." The minister smiled. "You will remember that he threw the moneychangers out of His Father's house?"

"Matthew 21, verse 12," Mother added helpfully.

"I remember," I said.

"Do you believe Mr Fairweather to be a God-fearing man?"

"I believe he attends church when he is on land." I was not sure how regularly he did so, or how strong his faith.

"He does attend," Mr Grieve confirmed. "I would say that Mr Kenneth Fairweather has the makings of a good man." Mr Grieve did not mention faithfulness. Perhaps that was not high in his estimation of a husband's essential traits. He leaned across the table. "It is up to you to enhance his good character further, Catriona, and ensure he remains on the right path."

I did not expect Mother to intervene then. "We have already discussed the other gentleman who is tipping his hat towards Catriona."

I closed my eyes, wondering what made mothers such awkward, interfering women. How much better the world would be if they allowed their daughters to live as they wished, rather than trying to help them.

"Mr Baird MacGillivray and Mr Fairweather were racing for the right to Catriona's hand," Mr Grieve said flatly.

I nodded.

"It is not a method of courting that I favour," Mr Grieve said.

"Nor do I," I agreed.

"Mr MacGillivray is a gentleman," Mother said. "He is polite, well-mannered and from a good background."

"That may be so," Mr Grieve looked over to me. "Do you wish this man for your husband, Catriona? His background and life are vastly different from your own."

"I wish that people would leave me alone," I replied tartly. "I did not ask for any men to make me the prize in their foolish contests."

While Mother looked shocked at my outburst, Mr Grieve gave a faint smile. "Quite so, Catriona. Men can be foolish in their pursuit of a woman. Sometimes they aim to impress while doing quite the opposite." Reaching across, he touched my sleeve. "Only the most sensible of women can penetrate the strong image men attempt to portray, to see the base metal beneath." He glanced at Mother. "Or sometimes the gold."

I was not sure what Mr Grieve meant by those words. Was he telling me that Kenny was base metal after lauding his Godliness? Or was he casting doubts on Baird, who had kept Mother and me off the streets? "I will try to remember that," I said.

"Good." Mr Grieve rose to leave. "I will see you both at the funeral."

"The funeral?" I must have looked astonished.

"You will not have heard," Mr Grieve said. "You were so concerned with racing on the Sabbath. Mr James Fairweather died this afternoon."

"Oh." I had nearly forgotten about Kenny's Uncle Jim. I nodded. Whatever my current dispute with Kenny, James Fairweather had been a good man and a friend of my Father's. I would attend the funeral out of respect for the man and to remember his life. That could be an awkward day, for Kenny would be there, but some things have to be done, however painful.

As was their custom, the women of the Fairweather family laid the body of Uncle Jim in his coffin in one room of their house to allow family and friends the opportunity to say farewell. Spread around the other rooms, men and women gathered in solemn conviviality, speaking in low tones of Jim and other family matters. I did not like such affairs, although it did allow people to give voice to their feelings and nobody thought ill of anybody who revealed their emotions at such a time. Even the Fairweather family, not the most demonstrative of people, were allowed some feelings when death arrived.

"Aye." Wearing her widow's weeds, Mrs James Fairweather stood beside her husband's coffin with a glass of whisky in her hand. "Aye, he wasnae all that bad a man, all things considered."

"Aye," Mrs Adams, the next-door-neighbour agreed. "He was always by your side, except when he was away."

Mrs Fairweather sipped her whisky. "That's true, Effie, that's true." She looked down on the face of her man. "He could be a cantankerous old goat at times, but there was no harm in him, no harm at all."

I drifted away, found a corner where I could stand and observe and said nothing. Mother was talking to Mr Grieve and I could not see Kenny, thank goodness. I presumed he was busy with his ship; Kenny was almost always busy with *Admiral Duncan*, and I hoped it choked him. Barbara was welcome to him and his blessed brig and its blessed sails and riggings and cargo manifests and all the other blessed nautical things that occupied his time and thoughts.

James Fairweather had lived in a detached house that sat four-square in a wynd, a narrow, curving lane off the Seagate, within a seagull's cry of the massed shipping of the docks. In common with most male Fairweathers, he had been a seaman, which meant that the majority of the people present were also of the sea. *What a wealth of experience is in this room;* I thought as I observed the solid, unpretentious, capable men and their thoughtful, patient women. These were Baltic traders, coaster skippers and mates, whaling masters, harpooners and boat steersmen, colliers and South-Spainers. The room was filled with seamen who had seen the world and who returned home to Dundee, and if I were to scratch them, salt-water would seep from their veins, mingled with tar and rum. I watched them ebb and flow around the rooms, talking, drinking, consoling each other, exchanging memories and anecdotes, and I wondered what my part in all this was.

"Thank you for coming, Catriona," Mrs James Fairweather appeared at my side, serene of face and with her eyes bright beneath a myriad of wrinkles. "Jim would have been pleased to see you."

"I always liked Mr Fairweather," I said cautiously.

"You'll be part of the family soon, I believe." Mrs James Fairweather surveyed me, no doubt wondering if I was suitable to join her crew.

"That could happen." I remained cautious.

"Aye," Mrs Fairweather stepped back, her scrutiny complete. "It could."

"I was sorry to hear about Mr Fairweather." I was unsure what to say.

"Aye. I ayeways thought the sea would take him, as it took your father. It's not right, somehow, for a Fairweather to die in his bed. The men don't belong on land, you see." Her gaze held mine as if she was trying to convey a message. "You'll learn," she added, and drifted away, solid as any battleship surviving life's storms.

I remained where I was when I saw Kenny enter the house. I could see at once that he had dressed in a hurry, with his coat hanging from his shoulders, and his hair requiring a good comb. A few weeks ago, I would have hustled him into a quiet corner to rectify matters, but this evening I said nothing, allowing him to look like nobody's bairn. He glanced around the gathering but either failed to see me in the crowd or chose to ignore me. Either way, we did not speak to each other as the number of people in that house increased. I had no idea that James Fairweather had been so popular, unless, I thought cynically, it was the prospect of free whisky and smuggled duty-free rum that lured so many seafaring men to the house.

"I hear you're going back to sea shortly," a whaling Fairweather shouted across to Kenny.

"The very next tide," Kenny replied and explained no more.

The whaling Fairweather looked out the window at the cloud-smeared sky. "Aye, the wind's kind for you."

"Aye," Kenny agreed.

"You'll miss the actual burial then," the whaling Fairweather said.

Kenny nodded. "Aye."

Although I was strangely pleased to hear that Kenny was as laconic with others as he was with me, I was dismayed he had not told me he was returning to sea so soon.

As the raw spirits flowed, the noise level in the house rose, with men roaring to be heard above their fellows, and women competing in equal measure. Yet, despite the racket and the alcohol, nobody appeared to lose their temper. I saw Mr Grieves moving among the crowd, greeting his parishioners as an equal and being treated with the respect his position demanded.

I looked up as I heard Kenny's raised voice. "I lost because somebody sawed through the damned oar!"

Frowning, for I had never heard Kenny shout while on land, I eased closer. He was in a circle of his extended family, with whiskered, weather-hardened faces and women in sensible, hard-wearing clothes nodding in solemn agreement.

"You mean that MacGillivray fellow cheated?" A stocky man asked, with his eyes like ice-chips and a mouth that would put a gin-trap to shame.

"Either him or one of his friends," Kenny said. "I tell you, the oar was sawn half through so it snapped on my return journey. There were holes in the bottom of the boat too, so I took in water."

I frowned. I could not imagine Baird stooping to such a level, but I had not been impressed with his companions. However, having a weakened oar would explain why Kenny came second in a race he should have won with ease. I took a deep breath. I now knew that Kenny had not deliberately lost the race. Perhaps I had been wrong? Perhaps Kenny still preferred me? I cannot deny the hope that surged through me.

With that thought in my head, I started when I saw Barbara appear. I did not know from whence she came. I only saw her sail through the Fairweathers, scudding like a schooner among collier-brigs, with her full top-hamper thrusting before her.

What the deuce is she doing here? I asked myself and dreaded to know the answer. When I saw her immediately steer towards Kenny, my heart sank. Until that moment, I had harboured some faint hope that I was somehow mistaken and Barbara's meeting with Kenny had been a singular circumstance, a coincidence or a misunderstanding. As soon as I saw Barbara heading for Kenny in this houseful of Fairweathers, I knew my hopes had sunk to meet Davy Jones at the bottom of the sea.

"Are you all right, Catriona?" The Reverend Grieve had clearly seen my consternation. Alone among his nautical flock, he did not have a glass in his hand or a glow on his face. He looked sober and solemn, as befitted his status and calling.

"I am, thank you," I said, watching Barbara engage Kenny in animated conversation, with Barbara doing the conversing and Kenny the nodding. When they moved away from the crowd, I made my excuses to the minister and surreptitiously followed, edging through the crowd.

Barbara and Kenny had stepped into the bedroom where James Fairweather lay at peace in his coffin. My intended and that arrogant, beautiful woman huddled together, examining something on a small table. I stood just within the door, watched for a moment that seemed to last for eternity, hating Barbara with an intensity of which I did not know I was capable, hating Kenny with an exquisite pain that twisted within my heart.

"Show it to your mother first," Barbara said. "See what she thinks of it."

Kenny seemed to consider the proposition for a long moment before he replied. "Aye," he said, back to his monosyllabic self. He lifted the object from the table.

"No," Barbara put her hand on his. "Not in front of everybody. Not yet. Bring her in here and show her."

Nodding, Kenny carefully placed whatever he had been holding back on the table and stalked, long-striding, out of the room while I backed quickly away to hide in a crowd of mourners. Barbara followed, barely glancing at the coffin.

The second Barbara left, I slipped into the room, trying to look solemn. "Sorry, Uncle Jim," I said.

Candlelight glinted on the object on the small table as I stepped over. I had been wrong – it was not a ring. It was a silver Luckenbooth brooch, with two intertwined hearts set under a crown, set with a central ruby surrounded by amber. I stared at it, instinctively knowing that Kenny had brought the amber back from the Baltic.

A Luckenbooth brooch was as much a symbol of betrothal as an engagement ring, with the additional advantage that it protected women from witchcraft, if one believes in such a thing. I thought briefly of Mother Faa and her strange advice. "Choose wisely," she had said. I lifted the brooch with my heart aching and replaced it; the touch seemed to burn a hole in my fingers.

It confirmed my worst fears. Kenny had given Barbara an engagement brooch and now was going to bring in his mother for her approval. I closed my eyes, trying to control the myriad emotions that surged through me. First was despair so intense I nearly swooned – I could feel myself swaying as I stood beside the table with that betraying broch on it. The second was a sickness I could not explain. I was almost physically sick. The third pushed the other two aside and forced away any lingering self-control I may still have retained. I was angry, not so much with Kenny and Barbara, but with fate for playing this cruel trick on me.

The anger boiled up from deep inside me. Lifting the brooch, I was tempted to throw the thing out of the window, but knowing that Kenny would soon find it in the garden; I tossed it inside the coffin instead. I know I was wrong. I know I had no right to interfere in an arrangement, yet I did it anyway and immediately slipped out of the room. Anger does that; it takes control, chases away all my sense and makes me act without thought.

I was standing innocently by the front door as my emotions stabilised, and I began to regret my actions when the tall, distinguished-looking Captain Jackman thrust into the house. "Mister Kenneth Fairweather!"

Three of the men turned around, including Kenny. "Captain Jackman?" I think everybody knew what Jackman's arrival meant.

Jackman nodded. "I apologise for interrupting this gathering, ladies and gentlemen, but I fear I must take Mr Fairweather away from you. The tide has turned, and I require him on board *Admiral Duncan*."

If Jackman had interrupted any similar gathering of landsmen, he would have immediately become an unpopular man, but to a clan of experienced seamen, his words made sense. The ship must come first.

"Coming, captain." Kenny glanced at me as if he had just seen me, opened his mouth to speak and closed it again. Although I could not read the expression in his eyes, I thought he might have wished to apologise.

Barbara's voice cut through the sudden hush. "I'll take care of the other thing, Mr Fairweather."

Ignoring the look Barbara threw at me, I slipped outside and walked away. I would not be rejoiced over. Any regrets I had about throwing the Luckenbooth brooch beside James Fairweather vanished. Let them find it if they could.

Dock Street was busy as always, with ships and seamen, carts and carriers, merchants and wives and all the hangers-on that the docks always attract. I hurried away, wishing I had never heard of Kenneth Fairweather, let alone got myself entangled with the man. It was apparent that Baird MacGillivray was far more suited to me, for he was a gentleman born, with money at his back and impeccable manners. Kenneth Fairweather, I assured myself, was a rogue, a blackguard and a scoundrel and I wanted nothing more to do with him. Anyway, I told myself, Baird had won both competitions with some ease.

Having made my decision, I should have been in a happier state of mind as I made my way home through the smoke-tainted streets. But, on the contrary, I was thinking more of Kenny's betrayal than of Baird's wealth and charm. The female heart is a fickle organ; it creates hope out of shadows and holds on to fanciful dreams despite hard evidence to the contrary.

"Miss Easson."

I heard the voice through a haze of my thoughts.

"Miss Easson."

The voice was female and insistent. I sighed; I did not wish anybody to bother me.

"Miss Easson."

I turned around, reluctant to speak and saw Barbara some 20 yards behind me and hurrying to catch up. For the life of me, I could not think what she possibly wanted with me.

"Yes, Miss MacGillivray?" I resisted the impulse to slap this woman, or worse.

"I think we have much to talk about," Barbara said.

"I can't think of a single thing I wish to say to you." I kept my voice as cold as possible.

Barbara stood a yard away. Half a head taller than me, and extremely statuesque, she was an impressive sight in the smoky atmosphere of a dull Dundee afternoon. She did not stir when a sudden gust of wind flapped her cloak around her legs.

"I think we have rather an important matter to discuss," Barbara said.

"What might that be, Miss MacGillivray?"

"The matter of a brooch," Barbara said.

"Could you mean the brooch that my former betrothed gave to you?" I countered Barbara's menace with a low, cold tone of my own. If this woman wished us to act like street-urchins, then I could accommodate her. Dealing with Anne and her friends in the mill had added iron to my blood.

Barbara looked confused for a moment, and then I saw a sudden flash in her eyes as if she had worked something out. "You foolish woman." she spoke quietly, almost with a hint of amusement which, if anything, heightened my anger. "You have grasped the wrong end of the stick entirely."

"What do you mean?" I asked.

"I can't tell you in the middle of the street." Barbara sounded almost friendly. "Is there somewhere we can exchange confidences?"

Unable to fathom her meaning, I nodded. "I live close by," I informed her. After visiting the palace that Barbara called home, I was almost ashamed to take her to our two-roomed house, but there seemed no choice in the matter. I certainly had no spare money to take her to a coffee shop, and respectable ladies would never enter a public house.

"Take me to your home then, Miss Easson, if you please."

With mother still at the funeral, our house was in darkness when we entered so I scratched a spark from my tinder-box and lit a candle. The yellow light pooled around the house as I carried the candle to the table. I knew that Barbara was staring around her, either amused or contemptuous or both.

Aye, I thought, *see how the real people live, not the privileged.*

"You read a lot of books," Barbara had noticed our bookshelves.

"Your brother observed the same." I was immediately defensive.

"And you play chess," Barbara said.

"Yes." *Why were my pastimes so important to the MacGillivrays?* "Sit down, do." I resolved to be as polite as possible to Barbara, at least until I found out what she was talking about.

We sat around the table with the candle adding its yellow glow to the light that seeped into our tiny window. I could hardly bear to look at Barbara.

"You have a comfortable house," Barbara said at last.

"You did not come here to talk about our house." I again resisted the urge to scratch her face, forcing what I hoped was a smile instead.

"No." Even sitting down, Barbara was an imposing presence. I could not fault her dignity, damn the woman. "I came here to talk about your betrothed."

"Which one?" Laced with bitterness, the words were out before I could stop myself. I saw what I thought was mockery in her eyes.

"The one named Kenneth Fairweather," Barbara said. "We may come to Baird later if you wish."

"I see," I said, although I felt as if I were swimming through mud in the middle of a fog. "Pray, what have you to tell me about Kenneth?"

With the candlelight reflected in her eyes, I could see the similarities between Barbara and Baird. Both shared the same height and overall presence, but where Baird seemed to find everything about life amusing, Barbara was the most serious-minded woman I had ever met, except perhaps the school teachers who had beaten knowledge into me as a child. If, indeed, those teachers were women and not demons in vaguely human form.

"He is your betrothed," Barbara stated.

I nodded.

"But you are in danger of losing him. You may already have lost him."

"I think you mean that you stole him from me!" Try as I might, I could not keep the heat from my voice as my temper threatened to retake control.

Barbara's mouth twitched in what she might have regarded as a smile as she shook her perfect head. "No, Miss Easson, I did not steal Mr Fairweather from you, and I have no intention of trying to steal him from you, although I must admit I have been tempted from time to time."

"I have seen you talking to him." I heard my words rush out as I half-rose from my chair. "I know he gave you a Luckenbooth brooch."

"You have seen us talking," Barbara admitted, "and we exchanged a brooch." When her smile broadened, she looked even more like her brother. There was the same near-mischievous glint in her eyes and the same whiteness of teeth against a face too tanned to be fashionable. "But it was I who gave the brooch to him."

"What?" Barbara's words made me more suspicious than ever. "Is that some foreign habit you learned in Hindustan?" I sat down with a slightly painful crash. "In this country, it is the man who gives a token of his affection to the lady, although she may respond with a lock of her hair or some such."

"I am well aware of the traditions." Barbara said. "Mr Fairweather asked me to make the brooch for him."

I stared at Barbara in utter confusion. "Why?"

She was smiling again, with the flame reflected in her eyes. "I am a jeweller, remember. Oh, not a shopkeeper with a vast stock to sell to the general public. It is a skill I learned in Hindustan, and I make specific items for people."

I vaguely remembered Mrs MacGillivray telling me about Barbara's pastimes on my first visit to Mysore House.

"Are you beginning to understand?" Barbara looked more relaxed now. "Mr Fairweather brought me some jewels, a ruby and some amber he had bought on his voyages, and asked me to make a Luckenbooth brooch with them." She leaned back in her seat, smiling now. "The brooch was for his intended, a token of his love for you." She gave a slight nod of her head on the final word.

"Oh." I stared at Barbara, wondering how I could have been such a fool. "Oh." I could think of nothing else to say.

"Oh, indeed," Barbara said. "You were watching when I showed Mr Fairweather the final result, after the alterations he requested to make it just perfect for you. I saw you hovering outside the door. We were going to show it to his mother when Captain Jackman called him to his ship, and then you entered the room."

I nodded, scarcely able to speak as I realised what a complete fool I had been.

"When I returned," Barbara said, "the brooch had vanished, so I presume you took it."

"Oh, dear Lord," I said as I finally realised the full implications of my impulsiveness. "No," I said. "I did not take it."

Barbara flinched. "You must have."

"No," I replied. "I threw it into the coffin."

For the first time since I had known her, Barbara's composure broke. "What?" All the laughter vanished from her eyes as she stared at me across the candle. "In the coffin? I put hours of work into that blessed brooch, and Kenneth paid good money for it. Do you realise he scoured the markets in Riga for amber and paid a king's ransom for the ruby?" Barbara shook her head in disbelief. "Do you realise what you've done?"

"Yes," I said, genuinely sorry for my impulsiveness. "If we hurry, we might get it back."

"We might," Barbara said. "Perhaps the old fellow isn't under the ground yet. Come, Miss Easson and let's put this wrong right."

"I do apologise," I said sincerely.

"So you should." Barbara stood up. "Come on, if we hurry, we might be able to catch the coffin before the lid is screwed down."

Blowing out the candle, I ushered Barbara out of the house and locked the door. Not for the first time, I cursed my evil temper and, not for the first time; I resolved to keep control of myself in future.

CHAPTER 11

DUNDEE, MAY 1827

The wind had risen as we spoke, so it fairly blasted us the second we emerged from the confines of Milne's Close into the Nethergate. We both grabbed our hats.

"I am sorry," I said again.

Barbara glanced at me coolly. "Unfortunately, your sorrow does not help," she said. She strode along in front of me, so I had to hurry to keep pace with her long legs. "It's not entirely your fault, Miss Easson. To be truthful, I knew you were watching us and rather played up to it, I'm afraid. Whenever I saw you watching, I would lean closer to Mr Fairweather." She seemed rather amused at her subterfuge. "I rather enjoyed toying with your emotions."

Once again, I felt like slapping this oh-so-clever woman. "Did you, indeed," I said.

"Yes, I did, indeed," Barbara replied. "I think Mr Fairweather is rather a fine man, Miss Easson, and I don't understand why you ever considered making him compete for your affection with my brother."

"I had no choice in that, as you know full well!"

We were hurrying along the Seagate now, speaking in short bursts as we stretched our legs.

"He's not as he appears, you know," Barbara said. "There are hidden depths to our Bairdie."

Our Bairdie? What a strange name to call the elegant, debonair Baird MacGillivray. "I was told that somebody sawed half through Kenny's oar. Might that have been Baird?"

"That wasn't Baird," Barbara said. "He's not as he appears, but he won't cheat in fair competition. Whoever did it, Baird knew nothing about it."

We were near James Fairweather's house in the Seagate now and slowed down, panting for breath. "Oh, Lord," I said despairingly.

The funeral cortège rolled past, with two black horses pulling the hearse and the mourners following solemnly behind.

"We're too late," I said. "The coffin's been screwed down."

"Maybe somebody found the brooch," Barbara said.

"If they have, they'll give it to you."

It was a forlorn hope. Nobody mentioned the brooch when we joined the procession, so we had the agonising experience of watching the sealed coffin at the front of the kirk as Mr Grieve led the funeral service. Then we had to follow the cortege into the churchyard, where Mr Grieve intoned the words of the committal ceremony before the coffin was lowered into a grave.

We stood there rigid, knowing that my brooch, Barbara's creation, was being buried with Kenny's Uncle Jim. With the rest of the mourners, I watched the gravediggers shovel earth into the grave, as the surrounding trees bent and whipped in the wind.

"What the devil do we do now?" Barbara asked. "Your Kenneth will never be able to afford more jewels for your brooch."

"More important than that," I said. "How can I tell Kenny?" I was more confused than ever.

The wind whipped our cloaks and coats around our legs and played merry-jack with hats and hair as the gravediggers went about their work. The Fairweathers stood in a solid mass, unmoved by wind and weather as I pondered what best to do. The answer came to me as the minister finished his service, and the gravediggers stood back, their job completed.

"Why, Miss MacGillivray," I said, "we act the part of sack-em-up-men and dig the coffin back up."

Despite the circumstances, I fear that I enjoyed the look of incredulous dismay that crossed Barbara's face.

CHAPTER 12

THE HOWFF, DUNDEE, MAY 1827

That was how we found ourselves in the Howff graveyard at 11 at night, digging furiously to rescue a brooch from a coffin. We crouched behind a gravestone as the lantern light bounced towards us, with the watcher singing to keep up his nerve and holding a cudgel in his left hand.

"If he catches us," Barbara whispered. "He'll think we're graverobbers."

"We are graverobbers," I said.

"Maybe if we explain what's happened, he'll help."

I looked at Barbara sideways. "What will you say? It's all right, my man, we're trying to dig up a grave to retrieve the brooch that I made for Catriona's sweetheart but which she threw in a coffin? Do you think they will believe you?"

Barbara shook her head. "No," she whispered.

The man with the lantern stopped and opened the shutter further, sending a broader beam of light across the tombstones. For a second, the shadow of the sleeping marble angel flitted across the grass, appearing to fly as the man shifted the lantern.

"I see you!" he shouted, freezing the blood in my veins.

Barbara gripped my arm, digging in her fingers. "Catriona!" That was the first time she had used my given name.

"Keep still." I pushed her back behind the gravestone as the light flicked past us, to settle on a bush that swayed madly in the steadily increasing wind.

"I see you, you grave-robbing blackguard!" The watchman lurched towards the bush, swinging his cudgel.

"Wait," I said as Barbara inched forward. Only when the watchman disappeared beyond us, and his lantern-light bounced away did I move again.

"I'm not doing it," Barbara announced, looking down at the partially exposed coffin. "I'm not opening it up."

"I will," I said.

Taking a deep breath, I crouched on top of Uncle Jim's coffin and then wondered what to do. I remembered hearing that the graverobbers would break open the end of the coffin to remove the body, so I pulled at the polished oak. I might as well have been trying to bite my way through.

"I'll have to smash the wood," I said, "or we give up and wave farewell to the brooch." I thought of the distress the loss would cause Kenny, lifted my spade and eased it into the joint between the end and side of the coffin. Glancing up, I saw the moon plain in the sky above, with the creaking of trees a sinister accompaniment. "Keep watch, Barbara," I said and levered to the left and right.

Nothing happened at first, so I increased the pressure and felt a slight give in the polished oak. Encouraged, I tried again, pushing harder, so the wood at the head of the coffin creaked with the strain.

"Sshh!" Barbara hissed. "That man is coming back."

I crouched in the bottom of the grave with soil slowly crumbling around me, and my spade wedged in the coffin. I felt, rather than heard, the footsteps on the ground. *Oh, Mother,* I thought, *if you could see your darling daughter now, you would have a fit with your leg in the air.*

"He's gone past," Barbara said, and I began again, trying to lever off the end of the coffin, with my tongue thrust from the corner of my mouth and my heart hammering. *Oh, please, God, don't let the watchers catch us*! I applied more pressure, feeling the wooden handle bend. I hoped my spade was sufficiently strong, closed my eyes and gave a hard pull. The coffin end finally came away with more of a groan than a crack, and I eased back with no real idea what to do next.

Crouching down, I peered inside the coffin, hoping to see the brooch. Instead, I saw the soles of Uncle Jim's feet. Unable to help myself, I gasped and recoiled.

"What's wrong?" Barbara hissed.

"Nothing." I steeled myself and looked again. *It's only a man. Dead men don't bite*!

"Do you want a candle?"

I did, of course, and Barbara dropped one down to me, with the tinder box following a moment later. Scratching a spark, I lit the wick and waited until the flame grew. Somehow the flickering light made things even eerier, with dancing shadows giving the impression of movement within the grave. Shielding the flame with my hand, I peered inside the coffin. I was very thankful that a shroud covered poor Uncle Jim for I had no desire to see his dead body. Closing my eyes, I reached inside the coffin and felt around, trying to avoid the corpse while searching for the brooch. There is something unnerving about touching a cold corpse, and although I knew it could not harm me, and James Fairweather had been a decent, even a kindly man, I would rather have been anywhere else but sharing his grave.

Oh, thank goodness. I felt something small and metallic and pulled back the brooch. "I've got it!" I heard the relief in my whisper.

"Thank God! Come up out of there."

"What about the body? We can't leave him like this!" I indicated the broken coffin. "Poor Uncle Jim."

"Leave him! The gravediggers will soon fix it."

That was true, and with more efficiency than we could ever manage. Dousing the candle flame and clutching the brooch in my right hand, I hauled myself out of the grave and rolled on to the damp turf.

"Halloa!" The call came from the direction of the watchtower. "I see you!" Lamplight probed towards us, distorted by the crazy antics of wind-tortured trees.

"Run!" Barbara said, lifted her skirt and dashed for the boundary wall. I followed, holding the brooch tightly in my hand. The things that we do for men! If we told them the half of it, they would never believe us.

The wall was taller than I remembered, with rounded coping stones at the top and the freedom of the streets beyond. Barbara was ahead of me, dragging herself up and rolling over the far side. Not being as tall, I was slower, and when I reached across the top of the wall, I heard a tremendous roar and felt the most amazing sting in my nether regions, the part of me that was then most prominent and most exposed to the graveyard.

The shock thrust me over the wall in an instant, so I landed in a flurry of skirts, arms and legs on the ground.

"Are you all right?" Barbara had waited for me. "Come on!"

"I think I've been shot." I put a hand on the place, feeling gingerly and gasping as I felt a rent in my skirt. The sting was awful, and I dreaded to think what damage I had suffered.

"What?" Barbara sounded shocked. "I heard the gun. Is it bad? Can you walk?"

"I can walk." I yelped as my fingers probed into my wound. "Come on."

Limping and with one hand behind me, I made what haste I could, listening to the shouts of triumph from the watchmen.

"I got one," somebody was shouting. "I saw him plain as I see you. He was a big, rough bearded fellow with a long cloak. I pinked him clean, too. He won't live long, I wager!"

"I saw them too," another voice claimed. "A whole host of them, half a dozen at least, but they ran quick enough when they saw me. They won't meddle with Wee Wullie Black again."

The voices faded as we moved away. I gasped with every step, with visions of a great gaping wound that leaked blood and would leave a trail for the watchers to follow. Thankful for the rain that had begun, I stopped to check the ground behind us.

"What's the matter? Have you dropped the brooch?" Barbara sounded worried.

"No. I've still got it." I could see no blood on the ground. Perhaps, I thought, perhaps my injuries were all internal. "Come on. We'll go to my house."

"I could take the brooch now," Barbara offered.

Ignoring her suggestion, for I felt that I deserved the brooch after all my work and pain, I limped the few hundred yards to Milne's Close, for Dundee is only a small, compact town, and thankfully eased inside the house. I was surprised to see my mother up and two candles lighting the interior.

"What's to do?" I saw Mother register my somewhat muddy and bedraggled appearance. "Where have you two been at this time of night?" She was much more like her old self as she instantly took control of the situation. "I've been worried sick about you!"

"We've been finding a brooch." I tried to hide my injury, but mother knew right away.

"Tell me about that later." She leaned closer to me. "What's the matter with you?"

"Somebody shot her," Barbara said before I could motion her to keep silent.

"What?" Mother responded with the most emotion I had seen from her since Father died. "Who shot you? Never mind now. Show me."

"It was the most embarrassing thing to have to lie face-down across the table as my mother and Barbara lifted my skirt to peruse that most prominent part of my person.

"I see," Mother said calmly. "It's hardly even a scratch – I don't know what all the fuss is about. You have a single lead pellet on the right side. We'll soon have that out."

"Mother!" I cringed as she poked and prodded at me, and gave a loud yelp as she squeezed out the offending shot.

"There we are," Mother announced in triumph and gave me the most stinging of slaps on the exposed place, so I yelled again. "Now, Catriona Sheila, you remain just where you are until I clean the hurt."

With no choice, I jumped like a child as mother poured some of our precious stock of whisky on to my already stinging wound.

"Oh, don't be a baby," Mother added another slap, to my significant discomfort and, no doubt, Barbara's amusement, then helped me to my feet. "Now, tell me what this is all about."

Starting at the beginning, I explained the history of the brooch and my false ideas about Kenny and Barbara.

"I see," Mother said when I stuttered to a halt, still unconsciously rubbing my behind. "You got hold of the wrong end of the stick entirely and thought Kenneth Fairweather was seeing another woman behind your back." With a glance at Barbara, Mother told me in no uncertain terms what she thought of my behaviour and what she would have done if I had been a few years younger.

I listened, red-faced and decidedly uncomfortable.

"All right, that's my piece said, and I won't mention it again." Mother nodded to me to signify that the matter was now closed, a fact for which I was extremely grateful. I know I was long past childhood, but the best of mothers have that effect on their children. It is not caused by fear of correction, rather by a fear of disappointing the person who has always loved you most.

"More important," Mother went on, "is how you are going to make amends to that young man."

"You mean make amends to Kenny?"

"I mean none other."

"There is also Mr MacGillivray to consider," I said.

"You need not consider Mr MacGillivray or a hundred Mr MacGillivrays," Mother said severely. "That man had no right to impose such a ridiculous competition on Mr Fairweather and even less right to manipulate you with his childish games." Mother's glare encompassed Barbara as if she had influenced Baird's decision. Barbara, for all her poise and elegance, remained quiet when Mother took charge. "No, Catriona, you have to make it up to that young man before you lose him for good. We can pay Mr MacGillivray back the money we owe him when we have it."

"My brother won't even notice the money," Barbara said. "He spends more than that on clothes every week."

"Good." Mother's nod closed that subject.

"How can I make it up to Kenny?" I asked. "He is probably halfway across the German Ocean by now and cursing the day he ever met me."

Mother shook her head. "Oh, you are a foolish woman sometimes, Catriona! Remember you're the daughter of a seafarer. Can't you feel the wind?"

"The wind?" I was very aware of the wind, which had been rising since the late afternoon and was now blowing a half gale, rattling the shutters of our single window.

"It's blowing from the north-east," Mother explained with little patience. "It's an onshore wind, Catriona, so *Admiral Duncan* is wind-bound in the Roads and will remain there until the weather moderates. He can only be half a mile from where you sit now."

I stared at Mother, still not fully comprehending what she meant. Onshore wind, offshore wind, what did it matter? Kenny was at sea, I was on land and that, to me, was the end of the matter. Mother sighed and leaned closer to me across the table. "Take a boat and go to him, woman! If you love your man, you must be prepared to work to keep him."

I looked down at my mud-stained clothing and felt the still-raging wound in my nether regions. Work to keep him? What did Mother think I had been doing to get in such a state?

"Take a boat?" I heard the disbelief in my voice. "If a ship like *Admiral Duncan* can't go to sea, how am I going to get out to her in a small boat?"

Mother sighed. "*Admiral Duncan* is riding out the storm. She is at anchor in Dundee Roads, quarter of a mile or so off Dundee, but she'll be there only until Captain Jackman deems it safe to leave." She looked me up and down. "Change into something more suitable and go to your man."

"I'm not going to sea," I said.

"Go to him," Mother ordered. "You won't go to sea. Just show him your love, hand him his brooch, explain what happened and come back." Her smile was a reminder of her beauty as a young woman. "Do you want to keep him?"

I thought of Kenny as a boy with his serious face, and as a youth when the sea had called him, and I thought of Baird's charm and polite manners. Both had their appeal, but I had always known Kenny while Baird was an unknown quantity who lived in a world where I did not belong. "I might have already lost him," I said. "He hardly talks to me."

"Do you want to keep him?" Mother repeated.

Glancing at Barbara, I nodded. "Yes."

"Then go to him," Mother said.

"But my work," I said. "I'll be late..."

"There are other jobs," Mother said. "Your man is more important than a job in Blackwood's Mill."

I considered that for only a moment and suddenly I realised that Mother was absolutely right. I took a deep breath. "All right," I said.

With the decision made, I was all scurry and bustle, changing from my grave-muddied clothes to something warm and decent, with my other pair of sensible boots on, a Fearnought coat that was anything but ladylike and a hat pulled firmly down against the weather. When I gasped as my wound troubled me, Mother merely snorted.

"You'll live," was all the sympathy she offered and then, when I was dressed suitable to explore the North Pole, she gave me a shove towards the door. "Go," she said. "Go and claim your man."

"Go on," Barbara encouraged, with a smile that might even have been genuine, and then I was outside in the close with the wind whistling around me and the moon only a faded memory.

"Wait," Barbara said. "I'll accompany you to the harbour."

It is no distance from Milne's Close to the dock, where the rigging of a dozen ships rattled and clinked together, and two or three late-coming seamen staggered along the quayside in imminent danger of falling into the water. A score of barges and boats bobbed alongside, some with oars, others without any means of propulsion.

I heard somebody singing from the fo'c'sle of a collier, the words too obscene for my sensitive ears, so I listened absently as I selected the best boat for my purposes. A neat little dinghy floated apart from the others, with the light from the collier's cabin reflecting on her paintwork.

Emily Kate, her name read, which was a homely name for a blue-and-white painted and trim little craft.

"She'll do," I said.

"Good luck," Barbara said as I manoeuvred down the seaweed-slippery steps towards *Emily Kate.*

"Thank you," I whispered. I found that after all my earlier doubts, I was beginning to like Barbara.

Emily Kate bounced before me, rising and falling on the slight swell within the dock. Pulling my Fearnought close around me, I took my seat, gasped anew as my damaged person made contact with the hard surface of the wood, untied the painter and pushed off. For a moment, I remembered happy days when Kenny and I had rowed boats as children, with our voices shrill and life all a game, but the reality returned, and I negotiated the ships at anchor. I saw a seaman standing at the stern of a coaster, ignored his hail and pulled on, rounding the counter of a Dutch vessel and headed for the entrance to the Tay. I know that women are not supposed to have the ability to do something as masculine as rowing a small boat, but that is all moonshine and nonsense. Women have been rowing boats since Naamah, Noah's wife, advised him how to sail the Ark, and anyway, I had grown up around the Tay.

The wind picked up the moment I cleared the harbour wall, and waves that had barely lifted *Emily Kate* now tossed her around and showered my back with hatfuls of spindrift. Ignoring the nagging pain where I sat down, I glanced over my shoulder to see the ships in the Roads. All wore their riding lights to warn others to keep clear, and I made out *Admiral Duncan* at once. I knew the shape of her masts, with that foreshortened mizzen that Kenny always claimed made her more manoeuvrable.

The sea was choppy, with the wind lifting spindrift from the wave-tops and tossing *Emily Kate* around as if she were a leaf. Gritting my teeth, I dug in the oars and pulled, heading for *Admiral Duncan.* One moment I was deep in the trough between two waves, and the next I was soaring high, with the wind biting at my ears and whipping my face. I pulled on, now determined to reach my objective and barely thinking what I would say when I found Kenny.

"Boat ahoy!" The warning roar came from *Admiral Duncan.* "Stand clear!"

"Ahoy." My voice barely penetrated the whine of the wind and slap of the sea.

"It's a wild night to be afloat." The voice sounded again.

"Aye." I pulled alongside, thankful for the shelter that the bulk of *Admiral Duncan* afforded me against the blast of the wind.

"Who are you?" the seaman asked, "and what's your business?"

"Catriona Easson," I shouted, "looking for Kenneth Fairweather."

"You're a woman!" the seaman shouted. "I thought you were a lad!"

"May I come aboard?"

"Catriona!" That was Kenny's voice, plain as day, as he joined the man on watch. "What the devil are you doing out here?"

That was not quite the reception for which I had hoped. "I came to see you."

"What in God's name for?" Kenny did not sound as pleased as I had hoped he would be. "We're readying for sea."

"I want to talk to you," I shouted, with my voice failing with the effort of shouting against the wind and sea.

"You'd better come on board then," Kenny said.

Boarding a brig in a lively sea while wearing a long skirt and a Fearnought coat is far from easy. Despite the early hour, half a dozen seamen gathered to watch the novel sight of a woman in their ship, with one elderly man complaining that I would bring bad luck and another grinning as he offered me a "chaw of baccy", and this was about three in the morning. I turned down his kind offer with a smile.

"Well, Catriona?" Kenny pushed through the crowd of seamen to hand me on board. He was not smiling.

"I need to talk to you," I said.

"We're casting off shortly," Kenny said. "Make it quick."

Once again, I wondered if I had made the correct choice. What had happened to the old Kenny, the friendly boy with whom I had grown up? I felt the brooch hard in my pocket as my shotgun wound began to throb unbearably. "I'll make it quick," I said softly, wondering where to start.

"All hands!" Captain Jackman's voice sounded from the stern of the brig. "All hands! Mr Fairweather! Stop gossiping to that blasted woman. We need to get this ship making way! The tide's turning and the wind's moderating.'

"I have to go," Kenny said. "You'd better get back ashore."

"No," I spoke to his memory as Kenny moved away, giving a string of orders that had seamen running all over the ship, hauling on ropes and weighing the anchor. It seemed to be the fashion on *Admiral Duncan* that sailors wore short jackets or no jackets at all, with trousers that were loose below the knees and remarkably tight around the hips, which was most entertaining. I was so intent on watching Kenny at work that I forgot where I was.

"Hey! Get out of the way!"

I leapt back as a rush of seamen charged past to do something nautical. I could see Kenny climbing up the ratlines of the mainmast, gesticulating and shouting simultaneously. He looked so capable that

I felt a surge of pride as if I owned him, and then a feeling in intense regret overcame me as I wondered how our relationship had gone sour.

I wish I could talk to that man. I wish that he spoke to me. Pushing the brooch deep into my pocket, I held it between forefinger and thumb, taking comfort from the fact that Kenny had ordered it made for me. *That must mean something*, I told myself.

"Hey, missus!" The seaman who had offered me tobacco gave me a friendly nudge. "Is that your boat?" He pointed over the side where Emily Kate bobbed a good two cables' length astern.

As I stared at *Emily Kate*, I was more astonished than crestfallen. My knots must have proved inadequate to the task, and without the dinghy, I seemed condemned to remain on *Admiral Duncan* for it was already too far to swim to Dundee.

"Captain Jackman will have to put back to let me ashore," I said.

"We're on the ebb tide," my tobacco-chewing seaman replied. "He couldn't even if he wished to. No, my gal, you're with us for the voyage, like it or not." He grinned at my evident discomfort. "Cheer up, my lass, the sea air will do wonders for your complexion and think of the tales you can tell your grandchildren!" Strangely enough, his words were of little comfort to me.

CHAPTER 13

GERMAN OCEAN, MAY 1827

I stared ahead, where an ugly line of breakers marked the shifting sand-banks that marked the entrance to the Firth of Tay, and which the local pilot was endeavouring to steer us around. *Admiral Duncan* dipped her nose, shipping green water that rushed the length of the deck, soaking my feet and ankles, before hissing out through the scuppers, then rose again as we approached the open sea. Ahead of us, the pilot was rowing like a madman, shouting orders to Captain Jackman, who translated for the benefit of the bearded helmsman.

I stood, feeling very lonely and out of place as *Admiral Duncan* eased out of the Firth of Tay and into the German Ocean. I knew I had no right to be there, I knew I was in the way, and I dreaded what Kenny might have to say about things.

In the event, Kenny did not have time to say anything for the next few hours as *Admiral Duncan* battered her way into the German Ocean in the face of a stiff breeze that kicked up spray and howled through the rigging like a hundred banshees.

"You can't stand there, missus," my tobacco-chewing friend said.

"You might get washed overboard if the weather gets boisterous. You'd better get down below."

I nodded, feeling extremely miserable and wishing that Kenny would at least take some notice of me. "Where will I go?"

"I can't rightly say, missus. We're not a passenger ship, so there's no space set aside for women." He scratched his head to aid his thought process. "Maybe best tell the captain you're aboard. He'll find out soon enough, anyway." He touched my shoulder. "You should have left when we was in the Roads, gal, but don't look so melancholy. The cap'n won't eat you."

I nodded and looked aft, where Captain Jackman was standing beside the helmsman. Taking a deep breath, I walked to him.

"Who the devil are you, and what are you still doing on my ship?" he demanded angrily.

I felt as if I was staring into the personification of bad temper. Captain Jackman's face was bright red with anger, his mouth pressed into a straight bar.

"I am Catriona Easson, sir." I was as polite as I could be. "I came on board to speak to Kenneth Fairweather, and my dinghy must have got itself untied."

"Mr Fairweather!" Captain Jackman's bellow must have been heard back in Dundee. "Come aft, Mr Fairweather!"

I stood as Kenneth ran towards us. He stopped when he saw me. "I thought you had left the ship."

"No," I said. "My dinghy came adrift."

"Mr Fairweather," Captain Jackman's voice was like ice breaking from an Arctic iceberg. "I believe this woman is yours."

I straightened my back, half-expecting a denial.

"Yes, sir," Kenny said, to my relief. "This lady is Miss Easson, my intended."

Thank you, Kenny, for these words. I could have kissed him.

"Do something with her," Captain Jackman ordered. "I don't want to see her on my deck again. I don't even want to see her ever again on this voyage, sir."

"Yes, Captain." Kenny turned to me. "Come on, Catriona, and we'll find somewhere safe to stow you."

"I'm sorry if I'm causing you trouble," I said, quite truthfully.

"You little idiot!" Kenny was not quite so diplomatic when we were out of the captain's hearing. "You should have left when I told you!"

"I tried," I said. "My boat came adrift."

Kenny looked at me, shaking his head. I felt sick at his disapproval. "Come on," he said, shoving open a hatch and swinging down a companionway to the deck below. It was dark, stuffy and stank of a hundred different smells, which was not quite the romantic seafaring life others may imagine.

"There's a cabin here." Kenny had to stoop to move around down here. He swung a small lantern that bounced faint light ahead, showing a rough-planked deck beneath and a low overhead above. Opening a small door, he ushered me into a tiny space, half-filled with rolls of canvas. "It's a sail locker," Kenny said. "You'll be safe here, and I'll leave you the lantern."

"Thank you." I could hardly say anything else, although the prospect of sitting alone in that tiny dark cell was not appealing.

"I'll have to leave you," Kenny said. And then he did something that made my entire expedition worthwhile. Leaning across me, he touched my arm. "Thank you for coming."

That was it. Only a single touch and four little words but they made so much difference. Oh, I have read books where the hero expresses his undying love for the heroine and lavishes her with compliments, flowers and praise. Well, that does not happen in the world of Dundee mariners. They are forthright, virtually wordless and about as romantic as a November squall in the German Ocean. In my case, after weeks of monosyllabic exchanges, Kenny's single phrase told me that, although I had evidently caused him trouble, he still cared. When you love your man, that is enough, and then, standing outside that sail locker in the madly tossing, creaking world of a Dundee brig, I realised that I still loved Kenny Fairweather and I always had.

With that happy knowledge in my mind, I stooped into the sail-locker, placed the lantern on a shelf, perched my still complaining nether parts on a bale of canvas and waited. I did not know how for how long I would have to wait or even what for, I only knew that everything would be all right. There is a lesson in that, for although I was well aware of the old saying that it is always darkest before the dawn, I had forgotten the converse, that when dawn is lightening the horizon, a storm can disrupt all one's plans. I should have listened to old Mother Faa.

After my long night in the cemetery followed by my early morning adventures on *Admiral Duncan*, it is not surprising that I slept. I could not remember actually falling asleep, only waking to the most terrible noise and the worst sensation of pitching and rolling that I had ever felt in my life.

"What's happening?" Scarcely able to keep my feet, I left the sail-locker and scrambled up the companionway to the deck above. No sooner had I dragged open the hatch than a cascade of cold water soaked me.

I looked out on a scene of utter chaos. What seemed to be the entire crew of the brig was running hither and yon, with the desk a mess of spars, lines, blocks and no end of other nautical paraphernalia that I could not even name.

"What's happened?" I asked anybody who would listen. But the crewmen were too busy to bother with me.

"Mizzen's down. Get you below where it's safe!" My tobacco-chewer stopped long enough to tell me, and then ran on with a hatchet in his hand.

"Where's the captain?" That was Kenny's voice, high and clear above the terrible noise. "Where's Captain Jackman?"

I could not hear a reply as *Admiral Duncan* heeled to the side with the broken mizzen mast, complete with sails and lines, dragging her over and into the terrifying greyness of the sea.

"Cut that raffle free!" Kenny pointed to a tangle of lines. Then he was everywhere, giving orders, sending men all over the ship, chopping at a line here, organising a group to shift a spar there, dragging a man free from danger somewhere else. Without knowing what to do, I could only watch, until I saw another tangle of cordage fall on top of the ship's boy, a tousle-headed youngster who could not have been more than 10 years old. He screamed, wriggling but helpless under the weight. As *Admiral Duncan* heeled further to the side, her rail dipped into the still churning water, and the mass of ropes slid down, taking the boy with it.

Holding on to the mainmast for support, I screamed, "Kenny!" and pointed to the boy, but the wind whipped away my voice. I looked around, desperate to catch somebody's attention. The tangle of lines was at the rail now with the boy struggling desperately to free himself. I saw the flash of a knife and saw, for one second, the terrible fear in his eyes.

Oh, God, send help to that poor lad!

I don't remember relaxing my grip of the mainmast. I only remember slithering down that steeply-angled deck with my heart in my mouth and my hands scrabbling on the scrubbed planks for purchase. The boy had stopped screaming and was gripping the rail with one hand, while he sawed at the rope with the other.

"Hold on!" I shouted, as if the lad had any intention of letting go and plunging into the sea.

I landed at the rail, fought my sickening fear and leaned towards the boy. Gripping the rail with my left hand, I tried to unravel the tangle of lines that enmeshed the boy, gasping and choking with every wave that swept over us. "Keep working," I urged as the boy sawed desperately at the wet ropes.

He said nothing, grunting as he worked and I succeeded in wrestling free one of the tangle of ropes from around his left leg. Another massive wave soaked us then, and when it subsided, I spat sea water from my mouth and carried on, fighting the lines. Between the two of us, we removed another, but the third and final was twisted round the boy's thigh and seemed to be made of iron. Neither my ragged fingernails nor the boy's knife made any impression.

"I can't cut it," the boy wailed as his resolve finally faltered.

"Take your trousers off!" I yelled as an idea struck me. "It might loosen the rope!"

The boy stared at me in shock and, foolishly shook his head. Exasperated at the stupidity of the male species, I reached over, slapped away his hand, and began to unbuckle his belt. "If you take down your trousers," I shouted, "the rope might slide free as well!"

I saw a light in his eyes as he realised the logic of my words, and he scrabbled feverishly at his belt. With the buckle unfastened he tried to work the sodden canvas around his hips, crying as *Admiral Duncan* heeled further over, edging us ever closer to the sea. I helped, ungently yanking at his trouser legs, not caring if it took the skin with it as long as the lad was free. At last, as another grey sea rose, the boy's trousers slipped away, with the rope tangling around his feet for an agonising moment before I pulled it away. The boy gasped and jerked his legs up, staring at me.

"Come on!" With the deck nearly vertical, it was all I could do to keep on board the brig. I found myself slipping and tried to wrap my foot around the rail. It was under water. The boy was at my side, gulping a mixture of air and water as the broken mizzen had heeled us near sideways in the sea and in danger of capsizing.

"Take my hand!" I shouted. Although I did not expect to help the boy, I thought he might be comforted by some human company.

"I'm not scared," he screamed, his eyes tightly shut.

"Of course not," I shouted. "You're a brave lad!" The boy's hand was cold and small within mine as *Admiral Duncan* heeled over at an impossible angle. It was evident that we were going over, and all my hopes and dreams would end in the cold water of the German Ocean. Holding on to the boy, I fought my fear. I was from a seafaring family; my father had drowned at sea, and my grandfather. Drowning was a natural end for an Easson.

"Got you!" I heard Kenny's voice as a steady hand clamped on to my shoulder. "Stay strong, my girl."

Despite our desperate situation, the knowledge that Kenny was there gave me strength. I felt him pulling at me and gripped the boy tighter than ever.

Admiral Duncan lurched, and sprang back upright. She righted herself in a massive display of surging water and crash of splintering spars. Although I did not know it then, Kenny had commanded a group of seamen to chop away the splintered mizzen mast that was dragging *Admiral Duncan* over. He had saved the ship and now was protecting me. "Come on Catty!" I can't remember Kenny ever calling me that before as he hauled me away from the rail to the relative security of the mainmast, where he dragged me to my feet.

Kenny's face pressed close to me, streaming with water, his eyes more concerned that I had ever known them yet alive with a light I had never seen before. I retained my grip on the boy's hand, nearly crushing his young bones in my efforts to save him.

"You're safe now, Catty," Kenny said, and, pushing me roughly against the mast, looped a line around my waist and tied it tight. "You too, young Davie! Look after my girl, now."

"Yes, Mr Fairweather!" Young Davie piped up. "I'm not scared, sir!"

"I never thought it for a second," Kenny said, with a wink for me. Stooping, he gave me a quick kiss, the first we had ever shared. "We're over the worst now, Catty," he had to shout above the continued roar of the wind. "I'll be back for you shortly."

By chopping away the remains of the mizzen mast, the men had brought *Admiral Duncan* back to an even keel, but the loss of the mast made her unwieldy. Every pitch pushed her bowsprit or stern into the sea, and every roll dipped her rails underwater. Tied to the mast, I could only watch as Kenny supervised the scurrying, working seamen.

With the tangle on the deck cleared, Kenny sent men aloft to check the remaining rigging on the mainmast while he brought up a spare spar from below and manoeuvred it to the splintered stump of the mizzen. I could not help but admire the seamen's skill as they hoisted the new spar into position and lashed it tightly with cables and the most intricate of knots, all in a heavy sea that threw us around like a drunken cork.

I had long lost track of the passage of time, but it was mid-afternoon before Kenny finished the essential work, and ordered the men to attach a new yard to the mizzen and created such a confusion of lines and yards as I had never seen before. From time to time Kenny would step over to me to ensure I was all right, touching my shoulder and talking to young Davie, even bringing a couple of lengths of canvas to shelter us from the worst of the weather.

"It shouldn't be long now," Kenny said, with the sweat drying on his face and the stubble dark on his normally clean-shaven chin.

I was near collapse when Kenny decided it was sufficiently safe to unfasten us from the mast. He had a large sail on the mainmast and a smaller one on the jury-mizzen, as he called it, so the motion of *Admiral Duncan* was much better balanced.

"Come on," Kenny held me as I drooped, for being tied to the mast of a gyrating ship is an exhausting experience. "Let's get you somewhere more comfortable. The captain's cabin is vacant now."

"Captain Jackman?" I asked.

"Gone." Kenny gave no more explanation and I did not press, for I knew the sea is like that; it gives with one hand and demands its due with both. I did not object as Kenny helped me aft.

The captain's cabin was not much larger than the length of a man, with a single bunk, a desk and a tiny, shuttered window. "I would have put you here earlier," Kenny said, "if there had not been two feet of water sloshing about."

At least the bunk was dry, with number six fine canvas laid on top. "See to Davie first," I said.

"We'll take him to the fo'c'sle," Kenny said. "His berth is there. Let me see to you. Are you hurt?"

I had never known Kenny to be so attentive. "Nothing major," I said.

"Let's see."

"No," I said, suddenly embarrassed. "No." I shook my head violently.

Kenny looked at me with his head to one side and a faint smile in his lips. "You're safe, Catriona," he said. "I promise you that you are always safe with me."

As I looked at him, I knew he was speaking the truth. "Yes," I capitulated. How much trust could I show him? "The ropes chafed me around the waist," I said. "It's not serious."

"You were limping as you crossed the deck," Kenny surprised me by saying. I had not thought he was so observant.

I coloured. "It's just a small thing."

"Where are you hurt?"

The thought of Kenny examining the part of me where the grave-watcher had shot me was disconcerting, to say the least. "It is unimportant."

"All right." Kenny did not press me, thankfully, for the idea of his seeing my wound was strangely uncomfortable.

"I am chafed here,' I indicated my middle, where the ropes had been.

"Goose fat," Kenny said at once. "I'll be back in a minute."

Kenny was as good as his word. My middle portion was stinging abominably as the salt water worked its way into the rough areas where the ropes had rubbed off the skin. Kenny looked at me for a significant minute.

"I can't do anything if you're all covered up," he said wryly.

"I can't take anything off with you standing there."

"No.' Kenny said. "You can't." An idea seemed to come to him. "You're soaking wet," he said. "That can't be good for you." Dashing away, he returned in a few moments with a small pile of clothes. "Change into these. I won't be long. There are things on deck that require my attention."

I stripped quickly, peeling off my wet clothes with gasps of discomfort. There was no mirror in the cabin, so I had to examine myself as best I could without such benefit. The ropes had left angry weals around my waist, breaking the skin in half a dozen places, while my other wound nipped abominably. Hearing footsteps outside, I looked at the clothes that Kenny had brought.

They were men's seafaring clothes, consisting of white canvas trousers and a loose canvas top. There were no underthings, of course, so I slipped on what was there a second before Kenny knocked at the door.

"Are you decent?"

"Yes," I said. "Come in."

He entered cautiously as if afraid I would be naked and looked relieved to see me covered up. "You look rather fetching like that." He admired me for a moment with his gaze running from the tumbled mess that was my hair to my bare feet.

"Why, thank you, sir." I dropped in a curtsey, gasping when all of my hurts protested at this sudden stretching of my battered body.

"Right." Kenny was all business again. "I have goosefat. Let me see where you are injured."

"I could put it on myself," I said.

"I know, but I want to, damn it." Kenny spoke softly, yet with an appealing intensity in his voice.

"Oh." I had never seen him like this before. I think I smiled. "Yes, Kenny."

"Lie on the bunk," Kenny ordered, "if it pleases you."

"It pleases me," I said, sliding face up on the bunk. I hesitated for only a moment before lifting the bottom of my canvas shirt.

Kenny's face was a picture of concentration as he examined me. "That must hurt," he said, and, very gently, smeared three fingers-full of goose fat where the rope had chafed my skin.

I jumped at the first touch. "That's cold!"

"Yes, sorry." Kenny was genuinely apologetic as he smeared the fat across my waist and sides. "Could you turn over?"

I did so, wincing, and lay as still as I could while Kenny applied the goose fat. Until that moment, I had not known that being injured had such a pleasurable side. "Don't you have a ship to sail?" I asked as Kenny took an inordinate amount of time attending to my minor hurts.

"Yes," he said at last.

"Then go and sail it," I said. "What are you doing, Kenneth Fairweather?"

Kenny hesitated before he spoke. "I was thinking that you suit men's clothing. Perhaps you should wear trousers more often."

I was glad I was face down so Kenny could not see me blush. I did not expect his sudden swoop or the kiss he placed on the crown of my head.

"I must leave you now, Catty. But I'll come back soon and check you are all right."

"Kenny," I said, but I spoke to a closed door. I touched the top of my head. That kiss eased all my discomfort fade into nothing.

I could only lie on the bunk for a short period, listening to Kenny barking orders above and experiencing the creaking and movement of *Admiral Duncan*. After a while, I rose, rubbed at the tender parts I had not shown to Kenny, and staggered on to the deck. We were sailing slowly on a grey sea, with the wind howling in the rigging and a collection of sails like Mother's washing day. Kenny stood at the stern, next to the bearded helmsman, and the crew rushed around hauling at ropes and adjusting the sails according to the shifting wind.

"How's Davie?" I tried to capture Kenny's attention.

"I haven't seen him. Old John was looking after him."

"Where's the fo'c'sle?"

"Up forrad," Kenny nodded to the bows. "Down the hatch."

The crew nodded to me as I lurched past, with one man touching his forehead. I found the hatch closed, but eased it open and limped down the companionway. The fo'c'sle was only twice as large as the captain's cabin but held eight men in an atmosphere an axe would have difficulty parting. Davie lay face down on top of a damp bunk, still dressed as I had left him.

"All right, Davie." I knelt at his side, nearly choking in the foul air. No wonder so many seamen suffered from consumption. "How are you?"

The poor wee mite was half-frozen, and the rope had chafed him far worse than it had me. Fetching the goose-fat from the cabin I had just vacated, I stripped Davie of his sodden clothes and rubbed the fat on every part of him that was raw. "Somebody should have done this already," I said. "Have you got dry clothes?"

Davie shook his head, his eyes huge.

"No, ship's boys won't have more than one set of clothes." I wondered what I could do to alleviate that problem in future. "All right, Davie, get under the covers and keep warm." It felt almost natural to tuck the little boy up and then return to the deck, wincing as my hurts played up.

Kenny stood where I had left him with the wind blowing his brown hair awry and his face intent.

"How is the younker?"

"Cold, wet and exhausted," I said, "but not badly hurt."

Kenny nodded. "He's a tough wee lad."

"He's too young to be at sea," I scolded.

"He's no younger than I was," Kenny replied, and I nodded, remembering Kenny's first trip with his Uncle Jim as shipmaster.

"He's still too young."

Kenny gave a faint smile as he checked aloft and shouted something that had men scurrying to haul on ropes that altered the angle of the yards. "I can't allow too much pressure on the sails in case it brings down both masts," he explained.

"Where are we headed?"

"We're headed back to Dundee. As well as taking the captain and the mizzen, that squall blew us well off course and out to sea. Old *Duncae* won't survive the crossing, so it's back to Dundee to refit."

"You look tired," I said. "You'd better get some rest."

Kenny shook his head. "No. Nobody else can navigate now Captain Jackman's gone." He gave a weary smile. "We'll be back tomorrow if this wind holds."

I suddenly realised I was hungry. "When did you last eat?" I asked.

Kenny shrugged. "The storm took the cook."

"I'll get something organised. Where's the galley?"

"Thank you, Catriona," Kenny looked genuinely grateful. "Aft, near the captain's cabin."

The galley was little more than a locker and it took me a while to get the fire lit and wash some of the pots, for the previous occupant had obviously had a rather slack idea of cleanliness. I was surprised at the quantity and quality of the food, so made up some hot pea soup and added ship's biscuit and cheese for everybody, with hot coffee and plenty of sugar. Honestly, I spoiled these seamen!

When Davie came in, 10 minutes after I started, he was dressed in his old, still-damp shirt, with the tails tied between his legs.

"Where are your trousers, Davie?" I asked.

"I lost them at the rail, Miss." He addressed me as if I were a school mistress, which made me feel very old.

"I had forgotten. Well, you can't run around showing off like that – you'll scare the seagulls. Wait here."

Running to the captain's cabin, I changed into my own clothes and brought back my seaman's trousers.

"Here, put these clothes on. They're far too big but a lot better than nothing." I supervised, of course, rolling up the trouser legs and looping a length of line around Davie's waist to act as a makeshift belt. I smiled at the end result. "How's that?"

He looked down at himself with a small smile. "Good, Miss, thank you."

"Your shirt is still damp," I said. I had him remove it, dried it off by the galley fire, then dragooned him as my helper and sent him out to feed the troops, or the crew in this case. Davie proved to be a willing helper, running around at my command with a big grin on his face.

"Now you take over here," I said, "and scour these pots." I carried Kenny's dinner to him in a metal canister and watched him drink his coffee. There is something very satisfying in watching a man eat a meal one has prepared. It seems to create a bond.

"Thank you." Kenny drank his coffee without moving from his position beside the wheel. "I didn't know I needed this."

"You did," I said primly.

We stood in silence while Kenny finished his meal. "You're a good woman, Catriona," he said at last, which was the highest praise I had ever heard him give.

"I was wondering if you even liked me." I broached the subject that had troubled me for some weeks.

Kenny spared me a frown. "Why would you think that?"

I took a deep breath. The storm we had survived had blown away some of my reserve. Kenny and I had gone through a significant experience together, so confessing my fears was less painful than it would have been only a day or so before.

"Firstly, I saw you with Barbara MacGillivray a couple of times. I thought you were shifting your affections to her."

Kenny pulled himself erect, staring at me. "How could you think that?"

"I was mistaken," I said.

"Aye." Kenny slipped back to inarticulacy. "You certainly were mistaken. I saw her on quite another matter which I won't tell you about just yet."

I fingered the brooch in my pocket, smiled inwardly and said nothing.

"You said firstly." Kenny's eyes were never still as he checked his command. "Was there something else?"

"Yes," I said. "You barely speak to me."

Kenny looked even more surprised at my words. "I'm speaking

now." He looked aloft again, checking the sails. I waited, knowing he had more to say. "I never know what to say to a woman."

"Even to me?" I asked. "We've known each other all our lives."

Kenny looked anywhere except at me. "Especially to you."

"Why is that?"

I expected the long silence. "Because you're important and I've nothing interesting to say. I will only bore you."

I felt as if Kenny was allowing me to see some part of him he had kept hidden, and I was not sure how to deal with this new vulnerability. It was my turn to look away when something sprang out of the water to land with a splash alongside. "Was that a dolphin?"

"Porpoise," Kenny said at once. "We often meet them here."

"How often?" I was glad to move on to a safer topic of conversation.

"Every trip, nearly," Kenny said. "There are three pods of them in this part of the German Ocean."

"How can you tell it's not the same pod?"

"They have their own personalities." Kenny pointed as the next porpoise jumped. "See that one? That's a male, and I call him Charlie."

"Why?"

"Because he looks like a Charlie," Kenny's eyes were never still as he checked the rigging and sails, and then looked all around at the sea and weather. "Do you see that white mark above his eyes?"

Waiting until the porpoises surfaced again, I saw a faint mark. "Yes, I see it."

"It's in the shape of the letter C, so that gave him his name."

I watched as the porpoises kept us company for a while, emerging from the sea, leaping through the air and submerging again. They were delightful creatures, playful even, and I grew quite fond of them before they disappeared. I did not comment on the smile that softened Kenny's mouth every time the porpoises appeared.

"Do you have any more animal friends out here?" I asked.

"Lots of them," Kenny seemed gratified that I was interested.

"Tell me." I was more pleased that Kenny was talking to me than concerned about the subject. "How about that bird there."' I nodded to a black-headed seagull that perched on the rail a few yards away. "What's her name?"

Kenny smiled. "I don't know that bird personally," he said.

"That's a surprise," I teased gently. "She's a black-headed gull, isn't she?"

"Aye," Kenny said. "Do you know why these birds have black heads?" He seemed slightly hesitant as if afraid I was going to mock him.

"No, indeed." I touched his arm, feeling the smooth bulge of hard muscle.

"They are sailormen who have drowned at sea," Kenny spoke without a hint of irony. "The blackness is the sins they have committed in life, and as they survive as a seagull, they pay for their sins and the black fades away. When there is no black left, they go to heaven."

"That's certainly reassuring." I wondered if my father was a black-headed gull, cleansing himself of sin before flying off to heaven. Perhaps he was that bird on the rail, watching over his errant daughter and wondering what the devil she was doing on board a brig in the middle of the German Ocean. I rather wondered that myself, until I looked again at Kenny and knew that there was nowhere else I would rather be.

"Other seamen turn into albatrosses." Now that Kenny had started, he seemed loath to stop. "Have you heard of the albatross?"

"I've read Samuel Taylor Coleridge's *Rime of the Ancient Mariner*," I was slightly nervous about admitting my scholarship, for many men are unhappy with women with a brain.

"That's a strange poem," Kenny said at once. "I have it in my cabin." He looked away and spoke softly.

"At length did cross an Albatross,

Thorough the fog it came;
As if it had been a Christian soul,
We hailed it in God's name."

Looking at me, Kenny clamped shut his mouth after that, as if I would think less of him for reading poetry, and I knew he had granted me access to another part of his soul.

I touched Kenny's arm again, squeezing. "We have similar tastes," I said. "Do you like other poetry?"

"Some," Kenny said, once he realised that I would not scoff at him for his literary choices. "I like Walter Scott's *Lady of the Lake* and *Lay of the Last Minstrel*."

It was my turn to quote poetry as I recited the opening stanzas of the *Last Minstrel*.

"The way was long; the wind was cold,
The Minstrel was infirm and old;
His withered cheek, and tresses grey,
Seemed to have known a better day;
The harp, his sole remaining joy
Was carried by an orphan boy."

Kenny joined in, with his voice audible only to me as he guided *Admiral Duncan* across the German Ocean with the wind providing musical accompaniment to our words.

"The last of all the bards was he,
Who sung of Border chivalry;
For, welladay! Their date was fled.
His tuneful brethren all were dead."

We looked at each other, with our voices strengthening as we both realised our minds and voices were as one. I think that was the first time we had smiled in unison as adults.

"And he, neglected and oppressed,
Wished to be with them, and at rest.
No more, on prancing palfrey borne,
He carolled, light as lark at morn;
No longer courted and caressed."

We both stopped on the same line, and we were silent for a minute as the wind shifted and Kenny ordered the sails to be trimmed again. After initially pitching, *Admiral Duncan* sailed smoothly towards so-far invisible Dundee beyond the horizon.

Even iron-hard seamen need rest, and I could see Kenny was growing tired, although when he smiled to me, I knew we had shared a few seconds of something precious. "Are you sure somebody else cannot take over for a while?"

"No," Kenny said firmly. "It's my duty."

That was plain enough. I resolved to stay at Kenny's side and keep him awake. At least the weather had moderated, making *Admiral Duncan's* movement a great deal easier. "How about those birds?" I pointed to a pair of black-and-white oystercatchers that circled above us. "Do you have names for them?"

"I don't know them individually," Kenny said at once, "although I do know that they mate for life." We grinned to each other. "I had a Hebridean seaman who called them *gillebridean*, which he said, are the servants of St Bride."

"Oh?"

"That fellow, Roderic MacNeil from Gigha, said that the oystercatcher used to guide St Bride around the Hebridean islands." Kenny glanced at me. "If you look at the oystercatcher a certain way, you can see a white cross on a black background, or maybe it was a black cross on a white background, I misremember which."

"Maybe these oystercatchers are guiding us to Dundee," I said.

"That could be so," Kenny said. "Animals and birds have more sense than people generally give them credit for."

Whether the oystercatchers were guiding us or not, they kept us company as the light faded and night crept across the sea. Kenny ordered the sea-lights to be lit, and we watched as the sun sank beneath the horizon. The light was strange, a band of silver-red lying parallel to the sea, topped by a glow that slowly dissipated into the darkness above.

"I've never seen a sunset at sea before." Lost in the immense beauty of the scene, I moved closer to Kenny. He responded so we were pressed together, hip to hip, as the sky blazed orange, then faded to purple-mauve in a spectacle so melancholic that I wished to walk into it and remain for ever, with Kenny at my side.

Kenny. Not Baird. I wanted Kenny.

My decisiveness surprised me. Out here, Kenny was in his element. He knew what to do and what to say. He was an older version of the confident wee boy with whom I had grown up. Out here on the sea, he could converse and share; out here, he was relaxed. I took a deep breath as the colours gradually faded, and velvet darkness descended, to be replaced by a sky more bright with stars than any I had ever seen.

"That's beautiful," I breathed.

"It is," Kenny agreed with some enthusiasm. "Wait until you see the Northern Lights at sea. Forget Walter Scott, Byron and Coleridge; the Merry Dancers are God's poetry written in the sky." He stopped, as if afraid he had said too much.

"Go on." I squeezed closer to him. "Don't stop."

"You'd love them," Kenny said. "I wish I could show them to you, and all the other wonders of the sea."

"Why can't you?" I asked.

"We'll be back in Dundee tomorrow," Kenny said. "I doubt if you'll ever be at sea with me again."

I swallowed hard. I felt as if I had just found the real Kenny, and once we were back in Dundee, I would lose him again. He would be at sea while I would be on land, where Kenny could not speak eloquently, and I could not reach him.

"Why not?" I tried to fight my plunge of despair.

"You are only on board because of a fluke of circumstances. A ship's mate cannot bring his girl on board. Only a shipmaster can bring his wife, and even then it is usually on longer voyages than to the Baltic."

"Oh." Although I knew that Kenny spoke the truth, the words still stung. I moved away slightly. I spoke without thought. "Could you work on land?"

"Doing what?" Kenny asked, with a small, almost sad, smile. "I've no skills apart from seafaring. I could not work in a mill or factory, or even in the shipyard."

I tried to imagine Kenny within the dusty, noisy confines of a mill, working with people such as Anne, and I looked up at the immense abyss of the sky, from where a million stars glistened down on us, each one an eye of God watching over his people. "No," I agreed. "You could never work in a mill."

We were silent for a while as the sea slapped at the hull of *Admiral Duncan* and some marine animal splashed nearby.

"A whale," Kenny informed me, "come to pay its respects."

"Will it attack us?"

"No. They are harmless creatures unless we attack them." Reaching across with his left hand, Kenny pulled me close once more. "I can't understand why people wish to hunt them."

"Nor can I," I agreed, truthfully. At that moment, when I had all of the attention that Kenny could spare from the ship, I was at peace with the entire world.

I stood happily there, held within the circle of Kenny's arm, as *Admiral Duncan* eased under her jury-rig across the German Ocean. Although I remained awake through the hours of darkness, we hardly said a word, and I had never spent a better night. I wanted that voyage to continue for ever with Kenny and me together on the ship and the sea and the wonders of nature all around.

"I don't want this to end," I said.

"Nor do I," Kenny told me, and I could have cried with happiness, or with the knowledge that soon we would be back in

Dundee and real life would begin again. Turning within his arms, I kissed him, soundly on the lips and he responded with a will. I had never been happier.

Well, Mother Faa, I said to myself, *you said there was a storm coming, and you were correct. Now I have come out the other side and life will be perfect.*

CHAPTER 14

DUNDEE, MAY 1827

"Land ho!" A lookout on the cross-trees called. "Land ahead."

Kenny was scrambling up the ratlines in seconds, all business and authority. "Steer east-south-east a quarter east," he roared, and *Admiral Duncan* altered course slightly, with spray rising from the bow and the oyster-catchers back above us. I longed to join Kenny up aloft, but the helmsman, now a young man with steady eyes, shook his head.

"Best not, miss," he advised. "The rigging is not as secure as it should be after the blow. You might lose your grip, and the cap'n wouldn't like that."

"The captain?" I thought of Captain Jackman.

"Mr Fairweather's acting captain now, Miss, until the owners appoint another."

Looking overboard at the heaving sea, I nodded. "Thank you, helmsman. I wouldn't like to do something the captain might not like."

Within 20 minutes I could see the grey smear of the Scottish coast. I did not wish to be back in Dundee, for I knew that something good was coming to an end. This last day had been a revelation – I had seen other sides to Kenny. I had seen him as the master of the ship, giving orders that kept us afloat and alive. I had seen his tender side with the wildlife, and I had a hint of his intellectual side with his knowledge of poetry. My Kenny was more than just a seaman, and I had fallen in love once more. I felt the brooch hard in my pocket and wondered if I should give it to Kenny, or if he might think I was pushing him too hard. As it happened, I did not have the opportunity to hand it over for a shipmaster is seldom busier than when docking his command.

Quite a crowd had gathered at the docks to see *Admiral Duncan* limp in, with people rowing out in small boats to stare at our battered appearance and a tight knot of wives waiting anxiously at the quayside desperate to see that their men were alive. As always when a ship arrived from foreign parts, Customs and Excise officers were first on board with a hundred questions for Kenny, with a representative of the owners not far behind. In all the bustle and confusion, I found myself alone once more. I fingered the brooch in my pocket, wondering when I could best mention it to Kenny, decided he would be heavily occupied for the next few hours and slipped ashore. Mother would be keen to hear what happened.

As soon as I left the docks, waves of tiredness came over me so that I swayed as I walked and I made heavy weather of the passage along Dock Street. Knowing Mother was already at work, I stepped into the draper's shop to tell her what had happened.

"You're safe, and back with Mr Fairweather." Mother looked quite jaunty. "That is all that matters. Now get home and get some sleep; you're dead on your feet."

I nodded, left the shop and nearly staggered down the Nethergate.

"Miss Easson!"

I looked up, dazed, wondering if people knew any name other than mine, and saw Baird smiling to me.

"I've been looking for you," he said.

"I'm sorry, Baird," I said. "I must get some sleep."

"You look exhausted," Baird agreed. "I shall convey you home." he indicated his carriage a few yards away.

At that second, the invitation was the most welcome I could conceive, for I doubt I could have walked another dozen yards. "I should be most grateful," I responded. I tumbled into the coach, closed my eyes and was asleep even before the driver slapped the reins on the rumps of his horses.

I awoke with the most amazing sense of well-being. My first thought was that *Admiral Duncan* was safely in port, and I was sleeping on the captain's bunk. My second was for Kenny, and my third was that the birds were singing sweetly this morning. Then I sat up and wondered where I was.

I remembered Baird kindly offering me a lift home, and I had a vague memory of getting in his coach. I had no memory of leaving, yet here I was, dressed in a very ornate nightshirt in a large soft bed that was certainly not my own.

The room was large and airy, with a late afternoon sun sending slanting rays to reflect on the brass ornaments on the wall opposite. I sat up with a jerk. I was in Mysore House, surrounded by exotic Indian furniture and ornamentation.

"Halloa!" I shouted out, rising from the bed. "Halloa!"

A maidservant entered the room at once, dropping in a low curtsey. "Good evening, Miss Easson."

"Good evening," I replied bewildered. "Could you fetch Mrs MacGillivray, please?"

"Certainly Miss," curtseying again, the maid withdrew as gracefully as she had entered.

Looking around the room, I could not see my clothes, so I retreated to the bed. I was sitting there in some perplexity when there was a tap on the door. "Come in."

Mrs MacGillivray entered, smiling. "My, you look a lot better now, Catriona. You looked so poorly when Baird carried you in that I feared for your health."

"Baird carried me in?"

"He did." Mrs MacGillivray perched herself on the edge of the bed and patted my arm. "He was most concerned about you."

"He was meant to be taking me home," I said.

"He has taken you home," Mrs MacGillivray surprised me by saying. "He thought it better to come here, where we can care for you, than to your house in Milne's Close where you would be alone."

I could see some sense in that statement, although I would rather be at home. "Please thank Baird for his consideration," I said. "I am most grateful to him."

"You will always be welcome here," Mrs MacGillivray said. "After all, this will be your home soon."

With my thoughts full of Kenny, I had pushed Baird's hopes and the result of that silly contest to the back of my mind. Now, both memories returned, and I realised that Mrs MacGillivray still expected me to marry her son.

"I am not formally engaged to Baird," I reminded, as tactfully as I could.

"That can soon be remedied," Mrs MacGillivray said brightly. "Why, we all know that you have an agreement. All you need to do is politely inform that sailor fellow that you are no longer interested in him, and accept Baird's hand." Her smile was so warm that I could not help liking this woman.

I tried to be diplomatic, wondering how I had got myself into this tangle. "Mr Fairweather is a good man. I would not wish to hurt him."

Mrs MacGillivray patted my arm again. "How good of you to think of Mr Fairweather's feelings, Catriona. I would have expected nothing less of you." She smiled fondly at me and leaned closer. "He will recover, Catriona. Of course, he will be disappointed to lose you. That is only natural, but he will soon find another girl, one more suited to his class and occupation than you are."

I frowned a little. "I am not sure what you mean, Mrs MacGillivray. In what manner am I unsuited to Mr Kenneth Fairweather's class and occupation?"

"Oh, my dear! You are the sweetest of things, aren't you?" For a second, I thought that Mrs MacGillivray was about to kiss me as she came ever closer. "There is no need for pretence with me, my dear, we know all about you. In what manner am I unsuited, indeed!" Mrs MacGillivray shook her head, laughing to herself at some private joke.

"What do you know?" I asked.

"Everything, Catriona. We know everything."

"That would not be hard," I argued. "There is not much to know."

Mrs MacGillivray laughed again. "You are the most modest of girls, aren't you? I am so glad that Baird came across you."

"I am not in the least modest," I said. "I speak only the truth when I say there is not much to know."

"Of course not, my dear Miss Easson." Mrs MacGillivray rose from the bedside. "I will send in a maid with some clothes for you."

"Thank you. Mrs MacGillivray, who undressed me?"

"Oh, my dear, the maids did." I saw bright laughter in Mrs MacGillivray's eyes. "Did you think I would permit Baird to do such a thing?"

"I rather hoped not," I said.

"No, indeed. There will be plenty of time for such games after you are married. Now," Mrs MacGillivray's expression changed. "Will you require help to dress?"

"No, thank you, Mrs MacGillivray. It is very kind of you, but I have been capable of dressing myself since I was two years old."

"I'll send in your clothes," Mrs MacGillivray patted my arm again and left.

The maid came within a minute, carrying a choice of clothing for me to wear. The first selection was my own clothes, nearly unrecognisable after they had been brushed, washed and pressed to perfection, with some expert needlewoman having repaired all the signs of wear and tear from the ship. The second selection was far more ornate with a near-oriental twist that I knew came from the MacGillivrays' time in India.

"Mrs MacGillivray sends her affection, Miss," the maid said, "and asks if you would prefer her choice of dress."

Although the exotic Indian clothes tempted me, I opted for my own, dowdy but familiar attire. "Please thank Mrs MacGillivray for me, and inform her that I will continue to wear my own clothes that she has so kindly washed." For one frantic moment, I thought I had lost the brooch until I felt it safe within my pocket.

When the maid bobbed again, I shook my head. "There's no need to curtsey to me every time you see me. I'm nothing special. My name is Catriona."

I am sure the maid thought I was fit for bedlam. "Oh, Miss," she gasped. "I could not call you that." She curtseyed again, perhaps to apologise for curtseying before, or to give herself a few seconds in which to think. "You are Mr Baird's young lady."

Not wishing to embarrass the maid further, I said no more as she withdrew, and hurriedly changed into my clothes before scurrying to search for Mrs MacGillivray.

"Ah, there you are!" Baird greeted me as soon as I left the room. Slightly disorientated, as I was in a part of the house I did not know, I just smiled at him.

"Yes," I said. "Thank you for looking after me. It was very thoughtful of you."

"I could do no less," Baird was as charming as ever as he gave a small bow. "I am slightly disappointed that you did not choose to wear the dress that mother selected for you."

"You have already done too much," I said. "I cannot impose on your hospitality much longer. I had better return home, or my mother will be beside herself with worry."

"There is no need." Baird's smile expanded further. "We have sent word of where you are to Mrs Easson. You may stay with us as long as you wish and dinner will be served shortly, Catriona."

I wished to go home, but how could I refuse such kindness, particularly when Baird still harboured hopes of a deeper attachment to me? I had to let the poor, generous fellow down gently. I curtseyed. "Thank you, Baird. I do not wish to abuse your hospitality."

"It is hardly an abuse of our hospitality." Baird said. "I have something to do, Catriona, so I must leave you to explore the house alone. When you hear the gong, please make your way to the dining room. You know where it is."

I curtseyed again and watched him walk elegantly away. Baird was indeed a polished, debonair man and I wondered anew why he should be interested in a mill girl, from Milne's Close, the daughter of a seaman. He turned as I watched him, gave me the lowest of bows and lifted a hand in salute.

"Listen for the gong," Baird reminded.

"I shall do," I promised.

I wondered if I should slip away and get home, but that would be a terrible way to treat these people who had offered me nothing but kindness. No, I decided, I had to tell Baird that he had to remove his hopes of marriage as I had reconciled my differences with Kenny. Fingering the brooch in my pocket, I felt dread at the thought of hurting Baird in such a manner. No, I shook my head. I had no choice. Kenny was my man, and anyway, Baird could find a far more suitable girl among the wealthy of Dundee. He could catch a sweetheart who was more used to elegant houses, balls and carriages than I ever was. It had been exciting and enjoyable, but that was all.

With my decision made, I resolved to enjoy my last visit to Mysore House, for I was sure Baird would never invite me back. However, determining an outcome and carrying it out are two different things, especially in such a complex place as the MacGillivray household.

The gong must have alerted the whole house. Although I was listening for it, the brassy boom took me by surprise; it was so loud and echoed through the house. I started, much to the consternation of a passing maid.

"It's all right, Miss." She put out a friendly hand to steady me but quickly withdrew it in case committing the heinous crime of touching somebody as important as my good self. "It's only the dinner gong."

Thanking the maid, I made my way to the dining room, with my heart pounding at the unpleasant prospect of disappointing Baird.

Taking a deep breath, I stepped into the room and a different world. Busy servants had reorganised the décor, transforming the room into an Indian palace, with a riot of colour in hanging silks, while a canopy hung from the ceiling. The table was set differently from anything I had seen before, with brass plates and cutlery, while the smell of jasmine and spices filled the air. I felt as if I had left old grey Scotland and journeyed to Hindustan.

"Come in, come in!" Mrs MacGillivray ushered me in with open arms and a big smile. "I know it's not what you're used to, but we do our poor best."

I thought of our small table in Milne's Close, where broth and bread made up our typical meals. "It's beautiful," I said.

"I hope the food is up to your usual standard," Mrs MacGillivray added.

I shifted uncomfortably, wondering if Mrs MacGillivray were mocking our poverty, and sat down at my place.

Mr and Mrs MacGillivray were there, with Baird and, a few moments late, as if to emphasise her independence, Barbara joined us. She looked at me oddly before sitting down. At a word from Mrs MacGillivray, that Indian music began again. I realised that everybody was wearing the finest and most exotic of costumes, as if we were indeed in Hindustan rather than in a humdrum Scottish town.

Everybody was looking at me and smiling. I tried to return the smiles, knowing I had to tell Baird that I was committed to Kenny.

"Well now, Catriona," Mrs MacGillivray said. "We're all back together again."

"Yes," I said. When I realised I was expected to say more, I added: "It's very nice."

"Do you wish us to continue to call you Catriona?" Mrs MacGillivray said.

"That's my name," I said. "Unless you prefer Miss Easson." I wondered uneasily why they all exchanged knowing glances and smiles at my words. "You have all been far too kind to me," I said. "I can't think what I have done to deserve such consideration."

"It was the least we could do for a *lady*." Baird's words caused loud laughter around the table, with only Barbara not joining in. Once again, she threw me a curious look, as if urging me to do something, although I could not think what.

"We know, you see," Mrs MacGillivray said.

I wondered if I had left Dundee and descended into bedlam, with that strange music in the background and this family with their incomprehensible comments. I gave a wan smile and wondered how I could tell Baird that I was set on marrying Kenny.

"When Baird collected you yesterday," Mr MacGillivray said, "you were coming from the *east*."

There was more laughter at that as if Mr MacGillivray had said something very witty.

"That candle is guttering," Baird pointed to a perfectly sound candle near the foot of the table. "It must be the *wick*."

That strange statement made everyone at the table howl with mirth, except for Barbara, who sat with her normal strained expression on her face. I sat in confusion, thankful when the soup arrived and I could concentrate on something other than their weak amusements.

"I hope you can adapt to our ways," Mrs MacGillivray said, "unless you wish to take Baird to your family home."

I stilled the thunder of my heart. "I must remind you that I am still engaged to Mr Fairweather." I had to force out the words, hoping I did not hurt Baird too deeply.

"The idea!" Mrs MacGillivray led the resulting laughter. "A

woman like you marrying a sailor." She glanced at her husband and laughed again. "We know, you see. You must have understood our earlier references."

"What do you know?" I asked in bewilderment.

"Everything," Baird said. "You can have no secrets from us, Miss Easson." Leaning forward, he snuffed out a candle. "Oh, my, I nearly burned my fingers on the *wick*."

For some reason, that second statement concerning a candle reduced the others to laughter again.

Sighing, I concentrated on my soup, wondering how I could convince them about Kenny. "You have all been more than generous to me," I said, "but I am committed to Mr Fairweather."

The knock on the door came as something of a relief in the awkward silence that followed my words. We all looked up as Henry the butler glided into the room with a card on a silver plate. "There is a gentleman to see Mr Baird MacGillivray."

"Oh?" Mr MacGillivray frowned, looking at Baird. "What sort of gentleman?"

Baird glanced at the card and raised his eyebrows. "It's a mister Abraham Anderson, factor to the Pitlunie Estate."

I frowned, for the name Pitlunie was vaguely familiar.

"Do you have any business interests there?" Mr MacGillivray asked.

"None that I know of," Baird replied. "Excuse me; I'll go and speak to this fellow. I won't be long."

"It'll be business," Mrs MacGillivray said to me as Baird left the room. "It's always business with Mr MacGillivray. You'll get used to it when you are married. All wives do."

"I don't think it will be the same with Mr Fairweather," I noticed that Barbara was watching me through narrowed eyes. Of them all, she was the quietest of the family. Even after our shared experiences in the Howff Graveyard, I was still unsure if I liked her or not.

Baird was back within 10 minutes with a twisted little smile on his face. "That was interesting," he said, sitting down with a significant look at me. "That gentleman was representing Miss Ogilvy of Pitlunie. She wishes to meet me on some matter. Mr Anderson was not clear what."

I nodded. I remembered a Miss Ogilvy of Pitlunie from the Provost's Ball. She had been unpleasant to me until Baird hinted I was a lady of position rather than a simple mill girl.

"Have you seen all of Mysore House, Catriona?" Mrs MacGillivray asked.

"I believe so, Mrs MacGillivray." I was relieved that nobody asked me about Kenny and hoped they had accepted my words.

"Did you see the east wing?" Mrs MacGillivray accompanied her query with a raised eyebrow and a smile.

"I think so," I said.

"We have installed a simple chapel there," Mrs MacGillivray said. "You will see it soon."

Barbara was looking at me very strangely now, giving small shakes of her head that I did not understand.

"I did not know you had a chapel," I said.

"I shall show you once we've finished the meal," Mrs MacGillivray said.

I had not seen the east wing of the house, and, if anything, it was even more ornate than the rest of the building, with intricate plasterwork on the ceilings, while candlelight reflected from a hundred pieces of brasswork. "Come, Catriona," Baird was obviously proud of his house. "You must see everything."

The MacGillivrays had decorated the wing in a mixture of British and Indian styles, with ornate tapestries and hanging carpets of the most gorgeous appearance merging with solid wood panelling and romantic landscapes that could have graced Walter Scott's Abbotsford itself.

Mrs MacGillivray guided me into a large, airy room lined with exotic weapons, the like of which I had never seen before. Strange, curved swords and long muskets vied for attention with suits of chain-armour and the most pretty pointed helmets. "This is the armoury," Mrs MacGillivray said. "Mr MacGillivray played some small part in the late Pindari War."

"I did not know that Mr MacGillivray had been a soldier," I said, with renewed respect, for the works of Sir Walter Scott had long awakened my interest in Scotland's martial traditions.

"Oh, good heavens no," Mrs MacGillivray said. "Mr MacGillivray is a merchant. He supplied the horses for a good proportion of the army and turned a healthy profit, let me assure you."

"A healthy profit," Baird echoed approvingly as if the love of money was to be worshipped rather than abhorred as the root of all evil.

"And in here," Mrs MacGillivray said, opening another door, "we have a different kind of room." She looked at me sideways. "I hope you like this place, Catherine."

"Catriona," I reminded her. "My name is Catriona."

I heard Baird's stifled laughter as Mrs MacGillivray nodded. "Of course; how silly of me, Catriona indeed."

"We call this the Love Nest," Mrs MacGillivray said as she opened the door.

I could not think of what to say. The most massive and ornate four-poster bed I had ever seen dominated the room, with a canopy of fine silk. Beyond the bed, the pictures on the wall would have made a marine blush, and the statuettes that decorated niches beside the pointed window were even worse. I looked away in some embarrassment.

"Do you like our room?" Mrs MacGillivray stopped beside a statue of a naked and very masculine man.

"I've never seen anything like this before." I was not sure where it was safe to look.

"Not in this country, anyway," Baird said.

I resolved to leave as soon as I could and never return. How could I ever have entertained any feelings of friendship for these people, with their lack of decorum?

Mrs MacGillivray was watching me with a smile on her face. "Next is the chapel. Come this way, Catherine."

"Catriona," I repeated. I was out of sorts after seeing that last room.

"This way."

I followed, feeling increasingly uncomfortable as Baird pressed ever closer, so his leg was touching my hip. I moved away, only to come against Mrs MacGillivray.

"Here we are!" Mrs MacGillivray stopped in front of a teak door, on which some skilled artisan had carved a Celtic cross. I barely had time to admire the impressive artistry when Baird pushed the door open and ushered me inside.

I do not know what I expected, perhaps something as outlandish as the Love Nest. I was very pleasantly surprised to find a small, neat room with a single arched window through which the evening sun highlighted the stained-glass image of an angel. Two short rows of pews faced a plain pulpit.

"It's lovely." I spoke without thought. Brought up Presbyterian, I preferred modest, straightforward churches without any fanciful decoration to distract from the minister's message.

Mrs MacGillivray nodded. "I hope that this chapel becomes part of the MacGillivray legacy." She raised her voice. "I want generation after generation of my family to marry here." Mrs MacGillivray faced me, with her eyes bright. "I will start a dynasty, Catherine, and you will be the progenitor of names that will live down the ages."

"Oh?' I did not want to say any more. I wished only to leave Mysore House and all the people who lived there.

'Begging your pardon, Mr Baird." The butler looked agitated as he approached us. "I am terribly sorry to disturb you, but now there is a young lady at the door asking for you."

"A young lady?" I felt Mrs MacGillivray's disapproval right away. "What sort of young lady, Henry? Mr Baird does not know any young ladies. Send her away. Send her away at once, with a flea in her ear!"

"I tried, Madam," Henry bowed to sweeten his words. "I told the young lady that Mr Baird is not to be disturbed, but she insisted, Madam. She said that Mr Baird knows her and she has intelligence that will be of great interest."

"Who is this insistent person?" Mrs MacGillivray asked.

Somehow I already knew the answer. "The young woman calls herself Miss Clarissa Ogilvy of Pitlunie," Henry said.

I thought of that elegant, long-nosed woman from the ball and wondered what trouble she was trying to create.

"I'll see her," Baird said. "Pray excuse me, Catriona." He made a short bow, to which I responded with an equally brief curtsey.

"Do you know this woman, Baird?" Mrs MacGillivray's voice could have cut through glass.

"We met at the Provost's Ball." Baird spoke over his shoulder. "It's all right, Mother. I'll get rid of her."

Mrs MacGillivray frowned. "Tell her that you already have a young lady. Tell her not to bother us again." She followed Baird step by step out of the east wing and into the main body of the house, giving advice every yard of the way. I followed, hoping I could make my excuses and leave while Miss Clarissa of the long nose occupied Baird.

"There's no need for you to concern yourself, my dear." Mrs MacGillivray eventually ceased her stream of advice to Baird and addressed me instead. "Baird and I will soon get rid of this Ogilvy woman." She patted my arm. "Now don't you fret. I'll make sure that Baird stays faithful to you."

"Mrs MacGillivray," I kept my temper with an effort, for the Love Nest had shaken me. "I am spoken for."

"I know that my dear," Mrs MacGillivray gave a conspiratorial smile. "You just wait in my boudoir while we deal with things." She ushered me into a most delightful room, light and airy, with large windows overlooking the Tay. I sat in a cane-bottomed chair, lifted one of the books that were scattered over an occasional table and pretended to leaf through the pages while I listened intently to hear what was happening. I confess that I contemplated following Mrs MacGillivray to listen outside the drawing room door but, with so many servants in the house, that was impossible.

I heard raised voices, with Mrs MacGillivray's to the fore. "How dare you! How dare you say such a thing?"

Baird spoke then, his timbre rich, fruity and filled with humour. "I think you'd better leave us, Miss Ogilvy."

"I tell you." That was a female voice, evidently Miss Ogilvy, "she is only a mill girl! She is not Lady Eastwick but an imposter."

I started up at that. I had suspected the conversation would concern me, and Miss Clarissa Ogilvy had no liking for me after our encounter at the ball. Well, on this occasion she was right, I *was* only a mill girl if never an imposter. I would have slipped away if the drawing room were not right beside the front door.

"Henry!" Mrs MacGillivray raised her voice once more. "Fetch the dogs, Henry, and fetch my whip! I will whip this impudent woman from our property!"

Unable to resist the temptation, I stepped down to watch the fun. I did not like Miss Clarissa Ogilvy so was nothing loath to watch Mrs MacGillivray throw her out of the house. In the event, Miss Ogilvy left before the arrival of either the dogs or the whip, although I did rather hope to see Mrs MacGillivray lay about her. Still, it was pleasant to see the high-and-mighty Clarissa humble herself by lifting her skirts above her elegantly-turned ankles and nearly, but not quite, run out of the open door and down the steps to her waiting carriage.

"Now, Catriona." Mrs MacGillivray faced me. "We have matters to discuss."

"Yes, Mrs MacGillivray." suddenly glad that Mrs MacGillivray was not holding her whip, I faced her squarely across half the width of the hall. I was determined not to be intimidated, or to back down from this woman, or anybody else.

"You'll stay the night here." Mrs MacGillivray was breathing heavily. "Now that we've got rid of that woman and her silly ideas, I'll keep you from harm." She smiled again. "It's quite all right, Catherine, you are safe here."

"I'm safe at home." I tried to push past. "I'd like to leave now, Mrs MacGillivray."

"No, no. We are trying to help you, Catherine." I found Henry behind me, with a couple of the older maids arriving in support. "You are not safe out there with creatures like that Ogilvy woman spreading her malicious rumours."

Despite my protests, the MacGillivrays and their servants hustled me into the bedroom I had previously occupied. Mrs MacGillivray continued to smile. "It's all right. We'll look after you."

With those parting words, she pushed the door shut. I heard the key turn in the lock and slumped onto the bed in frustration. *What the devil should I do now?*

CHAPTER 15

MYSORE HOUSE, MAY 1827

After my initial surprise, I began to plan my escape, for, however friendly the MacGillivrays were and however comfortable my quarters, I was undoubtedly a prisoner in Mysore House. Remembering that strange Love Nest of Mrs MacGillivray's, I shivered, for I did not doubt the use to which she intended to put it. For a moment, I blanched, imagining her standing over Baird and me, giving free advice as we lay together on that bed. No, oh, dear Lord, no. I banished that nightmare from my thoughts and concentrated on a more positive outcome.

I quickly opened the bedroom window and looked out, but I was two floors up and had never possessed any head for heights, or any inclination to become a cat burglar. I measured the distance to the ground, shivered and closed the window again. Climbing 40 feet down a smooth ashlar wall was not an option I could consider. I turned my attention to the door. It was securely locked and, when I knelt and peered through the key-hole, I could see the tip of the key still in place.

That gave me some hope. I had read in books that it was possible to unlock one's door by grasping the end of a key with long-nosed pliers or some other implement, and turning in the required direction. As I had no pliers, I searched the room for anything else that I could use.

When I found nothing, my frustration mounted. I tried the handle again, rattling it without any success. The door remained firmly closed, and I remained just as tightly trapped within that oh-so-comfortable room. Sitting back on the bed, I curled my hands into fists and beat them on my knees. After a few moments, I realised that I was only tiring myself out without achieving anything and stopped.

I heard gales of laughter from both Mrs MacGillivray and Baird, compared their amusement to my present situation and began to pace up and down the length of the room. Twice more, I tested the window, wondering if I could indeed try to climb down the wall to the ground below. No; I shook my head, I could not. I was not the heroine of some cheap romance, but an ordinary mill worker from Dundee. As the day faded, I found a candle, scraped a spark from the tinder box and watched until the flame steadied.

I don't know how or when I slept. I only know that I did not undress and nobody offered me warm water in which to wash. I must have slumped on to the bed in despair and allowed tiredness to take control of my body. Or perhaps it was a surfeit of nervous exhaustion that overtook me.

My door opened without even the warning of a rap and Barbara slipped in. "Catriona," she said, closing the door behind her. "We must talk."

I noticed that the candle was guttering, throwing only minimal light into the room, so I must have slept for some time. "I have questions to ask you, too," I said. "What was all the laughing and joking about at yesterday's meal? Do your people find me amusing? Don't they understand that I am not going to marry Baird?"

"Never mind that now," Barbara said. "I'm going to ask you a simple question, and please give me an honest answer."

"I always do," I said.

"Sit down," Barbara said, "and look at me."

I had never seen Barbara look so serious as I sat on a luxuriously padded chair. "What's the matter, Barbara?"

Barbara crouched in front of me and took hold of my hands. "Now Catriona, dear Catriona, please tell me: what is your real name?"

"Why, Barbara, my real name is Catriona Easson."

"Is that the name you were born with?"

"Yes," I said, bewildered.

"What is your mother's name?"

I frowned. "Fiona Easson. Her maiden name was Fiona Armstrong. Why all these questions, Barbara?"

Barbara seemed to relax with each answer I gave her. "Have you ever been Catherine Eastwick?"

I shook my head. "No. But the name is familiar. I think that Ogilvy woman mentioned it."

" Lady Catherine Eastwick is the heir to Eastwick Hall."

"Oh." I shrugged in confusion.

"Don't you read the society and scandal columns in the paper?" Barbara asked.

I shook my head. "No."

"Oh." Barbara looked surprised. "You miss some juicy tit-bits of intelligence." Frowning, she explained further: "Lady Catherine Eastwick has been missing since her father the earl drowned in a boating accident and she inherited Eastwick Hall and the family fortune. There were reports that she was overwhelmed by suitors hoping to marry her and get hold of her inheritance, and my mother and my idiot of a brother think you are Lady Eastwick."

"Dear God!" I remembered the weak "wick" and "east" jokes, and the way Mrs MacGillivray constantly addressed me as "Catherine". "What on earth made them think I was Lady Eastwick?"

"Lady Eastwick was reported missing in all the papers the day before Baird met you walking on the road to Dundee. Some reports said that she was going to hide in Dundee with one of her older servants."

"I think I saw some mention of her in the papers," I said.

"That's what sparked his interest in you, Catriona," Barbara said. "That's why he wants to marry you."

"Baird's been to my house," I shook my head at the stupidity of people who only believed what they wanted to think, rather than the evidence of their senses. "He's met my mother. He knows where I work."

"I know," Barbara said. "Baird and my mother believe that your mother is the aged retainer mentioned in the newspaper report, and you work in the mill to hide your real identity."

"Good Lord." I shook my head in bemusement. "That's utter nonsense."

"Good Lord indeed," Barbara said. "Baird also saw your intellectual pursuits, the books and chess set."

"My father was the mate of a merchant ship," I said. "He insisted that we, his daughters, should all strive to improve ourselves."

Barbara nodded. "I believe you," she said, smiling. "No lady would try to talk to the servants as you did."

I was not sure what to think. Part of me felt very insulted that Baird had wished to marry a titled lady rather than me, and part was relieved. "Oh," I said at last. "Well, you of all people know that I am betrothed to Kenny. All I have to do is tell Baird that I am not Lady Eastwick, and if you support me, all the confusion will be over."

"I hope so," Barbara said. "I absolutely hope so."

"I'll tell him now," I said. "Where is he? Is he still awake?"

"Oh, he'll be awake for hours yet. The MacGillivrays never retire early."

Baird was with Mrs MacGillivray in the drawing-room, scanning the financial section of the newspaper and sipping a glass of port. Both looked up as I entered. "Why, come in, Catriona." Baird was all smiles, as always, while Mrs MacGillivray acted as if it were perfectly normal to lock a guest in her room.

"Thank you." I stood beside the closed door, nerving myself for the statement I had to make. "Baird, Mrs MacGillivray, I think you are labouring under a misapprehension concerning my identity."

Mrs MacGillivray put down the intricate embroidery on which she had been working. "Why, no, dear," she said. "We know exactly who you are, don't we, Baird?"

"Yes, we do," Baird said.

"It's all resolved," Mrs MacGillivray said. "I have arranged for a church minister to call tomorrow and we'll have you married in our private chapel, after which you will be perfectly safe."

"I'm not Lady Catherine Eastwick," I said.

Lady MacGillivray laughed. "Of course not, dear." She smiled. "It's all right, Lady Catherine. Your secret is safe. Once you are married to our Baird, we can announce the truth to the world."

"I am Catriona Easson." I kept my patience for, despite all that had happened, I still harboured a certain regard for Mrs MacGillivray.

"Once you are married to Baird, he will take the title of Baird MacGillivray, Lord Eastwick, so our family will protect you from any trouble, and the MacGillivrays will rise to their proper position, with a title." Mrs MacGillivray smiled as if I had not spoken. "I have already remarked that you have fine childbearing hips, Catherine. You will ensure that the family line continues."

I stared at Mrs MacGillivray. I knew from my reading that a man is not ennobled by marrying a titled wife but I was more concerned with her more physical plans for me. "I am not a cow to be used for breeding."

"Of course not, dear," Mrs MacGillivray replied. "You are Lady Eastwick."

"I am Catriona Easson," I said, "and I am now going home."

I left that room far quicker than I had entered, with my head up, and my temper rising rapidly. I heard the door crash open, and Baird followed.

"Catriona! Catherine! Wait!"

I was not inclined to wait. Shrugging off Baird's hand, I strode for the front door with my breathing ragged and my skirt snapping against my shins with every step.

"Catriona, please!" Baird stepped in front of me, blocking my passage. For the first time, I felt afraid. "Let me talk to you."

"I've said all I'm going to say, Mr MacGillivray. Please step out of my way."

"We must talk."

"Mr MacGillivray." I stepped back, hoping to find some space. "I have said all I am going to say. I am betrothed to Mr Fairweather, and I will be marrying him. I am immensely grateful for the kindness you have shown me in the past, but that is no reason to marry you."

"I love you, Catriona," Baird said.

I stared at him. "No, Baird. Please step aside."

"I know you are not Lady Whatshername," Baird said. "I've known that for some time."

"I am spoken for." I still did not dislike Baird, who had always acted like a perfect gentleman to me. "Baird, you are a handsome, personable man. You can find a woman far more suitable than I am."

"I don't want another woman, Catriona. I want you."

Perhaps it was the way he said them, but Baird's words unsettled me. I believed them to be true. "I am sorry, Baird, but it cannot be. I am spoken for and will marry Kenny Fairweather."

"No, my dear. You will marry Baird." Mrs MacGillivray's voice came from behind me, and her arms closed around my shoulders.

Baird cut off my attempt to scream with a hand clamped over my mouth. "It's all right, Catriona; it's all right. I'm here and I love you."

"No!" I tried to struggle, but with Mrs MacGillivray holding me, Baird grasped my flailing legs and they carried me to the bedroom I had just vacated and placed me, very gently, on the bed.

"It's all right," Mrs MacGillivray soothed. "Just one more night and you'll be part of the family. You'll be a MacGillivray, too, one of us." Stooping, she kissed me softly on the crown of my head. "You'll be fine, Catherine. You'll see."

Forcing Baird's hand from my mouth, I shouted. "You can't do this."

"It's all arranged," Mrs MacGillivray said. "Remember? Our Bairdie won you fair and square."

"He did not," I said. "Baird cheated. He sawed through Mr Fairweather's oar so he could not row his boat properly."

"Oh no, dear," Mrs MacGillivray shook her immaculate head. "Baird had nothing to do with that."

I believed her. "Who did, then?"

"That was me, dear Catherine." Mrs MacGillivray smiled down on me. "All's fair in love and war."

"Mother!" I heard the hostility in Baird's voice. "You should not have done that."

"Of course I should," Mrs MacGillivray argued. "Look what a lovely prize I won for you." She looked at me. "And you, Catherine, look at my Bairdie. You will marry him tomorrow." Her smile was as broad as ever. "I have the most delightful wedding dress for you, Catherine. You will love it."

"I'm not marrying Baird," I said.

They both laughed, as at the tantrums of a child.

"What a temper your sweetheart has." Mrs MacGillivray addressed Baird. "But what fun you'll have controlling her."

I nearly spat blood at the words. "Fun? I'll show you fun!"

"We'd better ensure she doesn't hurt herself," Mrs MacGillivray said. "I've never seen such a display of ill-humour!"

"She'll be all right," Baird said. "Won't you, Catriona?"

"Let me go, and I'll soon show you!" I yelled.

"What a passionate nature your girl has!" Mrs MacGillivray marvelled. "She will undoubtedly keep us well entertained in the long winter nights."

"Lie still, Catriona, please be sensible," Baird pleaded with concern in his eyes.

Rather than lie sensibly still, I continued to kick and struggle, which was not a good idea.

"She will hurt herself in her passion," Mrs MacGillivray observed.

"What can we do?" Baird turned to his mother for help.

"We have to keep her safe," Mrs MacGillivray said. "You do understand, Catherine, don't you? We're doing this for your own good."

I glared at her, with my mind promising things that my hands could not then deliver. I did not see where Baird produced the cord from. I only knew he wrapped it around my ankles, smiling and mouthing smooth words as he tied me tight. My wrists were next, with Mrs MacGillivray giving motherly advice as she stroked my hair and kissed my head again.

"It's all for the best, Catherine, you'll see. We're doing this for your sake. Soon you'll be safe within the family, and we'll care for you the rest of your life."

Naturally, Baird had to remove his hand from my mouth to tie me, so I gave full vent to my feelings, telling them in no uncertain manner what I thought of them and their actions. "You can't marry me against my will," I finished, "and you can't keep me here for ever."

"Oh, what a temper!" Mrs MacGillivray seemed delighted at my outburst. "Oh, what a lively wife you will be!" She laughed again. "We won't keep you here, Catherine, dear. Oh, no. Mr MacGillivray has already arranged that. As soon as you and Bairdie are married, the two of you will board a ship for India. Baird will be our agent on the Hooghly, and you'll be at his side, as a good wife should."

When I opened my mouth to respond, Baird stuffed something past my teeth and tied it with a ribbon so I could only glare at them both, wriggling on the bed.

"There, now," Mrs MacGillivray looked fondly down on me. "I've never seen such a display of passion." She shook her head. "You get to sleep now, dear Catherine. You have a busy day tomorrow and then your wedding night." She looked at Baird with a smile. "After that, it's off to India and your new life with your husband." She patted my hip fondly. "We'll pray for lots of babies for you both."

Baird was still smiling as he closed the door behind him. I heard the key turn in the lock, and I swear that if fury could break bonds, I would have turned Mysore House into dust and rubble before five minutes had passed. As it was, I wriggled and wrestled and mouthed terrible insults, yet all my activity only served to tire me out without loosening either my bonds or my gag in the slightest. At last, worn out and furious, I lay on that rumpled bed with my heart hammering and my brain crammed with terrible images of the fate that Mrs MacGillivray had promised me.

It was hard to believe that while I would be undergoing the horror of tomorrow's forced marriage, Dundee would be going about its normal business. Anne and her cronies would work at their looms, dockers would load and unload ships, carriers would swear and shout as they drove their carts and, somewhere, poor Kenny would wonder where I might be.

After my initial fruitless struggles, I lay still for a while to assess my situation. I did not doubt that Mrs MacGillivray meant every word she had said. She would see me married to Baird tomorrow in their private chapel, then would come the wedding night, and I shivered at that prospect. I again had that nightmare vision of Mrs MacGillivray supervising the proceedings, standing in the bedroom advising her smiling son. I shook away the thought although the aftermath was scarcely less inviting, a ship to India and the life of a wife and breeding machine up the Hooghly, wherever and whatever that was.

No. I shook my head. I could not and would not submit to that. The marriage would be a sham, for forced marriages were illegal, so I could escape any time; but then, who would want me after the wedding night? What respectable man would want anything to do with me?

The horror of my situation returned, and I lay on that bed in frustration, wrestling with my bonds and succeeding only in making them tighter.

I have read books where "with one bound Jack was free" or where the victim managed to wriggle clear of her bonds, squeeze out a conveniently open window and release herself with the help of a handy handsome man. Unfortunately, the reality is somewhat different. I am not named Jack, I could not untie my bonds, the drop from the window was too considerable to contemplate and there were no handsome men within reach. And lying tied up is thoroughly uncomfortable. One gets cramp, the blood does not adequately reach the hands and feet, which swell up, one gets the most annoying itch in the small of one's back and one's bladder seems to know it cannot be relieved. It is the most abominably wearisome condition, and when one's gag swells as well, one feels as if one is choking, or at least this one did. I was not a happy Catriona as I lay on that soft bed contemplating my future.

I gave way to tears that did me no good at all and only served to add another discomfort to my captivity.

I heard the sound of the key turning in the lock. I dreaded that it might be the morning of my wedding day.

Candlelight pooled around me. I looked up and saw Barbara's face, half in shadow.

"What have they done to you?" she asked wonderingly as she looked down at me.

I could not answer until Barbara loosened my gag and worked on my bonds.

"Hold still," Barbara said. "They've no right to tie you up like this."

"They're going to marry me to Baird tomorrow,' I told her. For a moment, I contemplated dashing past Barbara and running through the house.

"I heard," Barbara replied grimly. "I'm getting you out of here."

"Why? I didn't even think you liked me."

"I don't like you," Barbara said. "But Kenneth Fairweather does."

"And you like Kenny," I said.

"I do." Barbara rubbed my legs to help restore my circulation, for I could hardly walk after being tied up. "Come with me."

My shotgun wound gave me a sudden stab of pain so, rubbing my rear, I followed Barbara out of the room, while her candle sent yellow light ahead of us and cast weird shadows from the grotesque Indian carvings that decorated the walls. I was about to ask where we were going but I kept my mouth shut for fear that I might awaken other people in the house.

Barbara led me towards the back of the house, through a heavy door and down a flight of bare stone stairs. "The servants' stairway," Barbara explained in a low voice. "The front door is locked and barred. There is no way out there, and there are shutters and bars on all the ground-floor windows."

I nodded, remembering seeing the bars when first I came to Mysore House.

"You'll have to leave by the water-gate," Barbara informed me. "It's the best I can do for you."

"The water-gate? Is there a path?"

"No." When Barbara stopped, I wondered what she had planned. "I'm going to show you something first. You might think differently about our Bairdie after that."

Again, I followed Barbara as she slipped through a small door and into a chamber – I would hesitate to call it a room – with stone flags on the ground and bare, un-plastered stone walls. With barely sufficient space for us both to stand, Barbara squeezed me towards the far wall. "Look through that gap," she instructed me, "and tell me what you can see."

I saw nothing until my eyes grew accustomed to the dark, and then I realised I was peering into the kitchen where Mrs MacGillivray had taken me on that first day in Mysore House.

"Do you understand?" Barbara's voice was gently mocking.

"No," I admitted.

"When my oh-so-caring mother brought you down here to get your clothes washed, she was making sure that you were suitable wife material for Baird."

I remembered Mrs MacGillivray commenting on my childbearing abilities as I stood in that kitchen. "Oh," I said.

"Baird was standing where you are now."

Barbara's seven words chilled me. "What?"

"Baird was watching you."

The thought of any man spying on me as I stood naked was terrifying but the idea that Mrs MacGillivray had conspired with her son to see me in that condition made me feel dizzy.

"Where's the water-gate?" I had to get away. I could not bear to stay one minute longer in Mysore House with its scheming, smiling, devious people.

"This way."

I moved faster now, nearly pushing Barbara in front of me in my haste to escape from that place. No longer descending stairs, we emerged into the garden that encircled the house, where a cool breeze eased from the Tay to whimper in the delicate trees. Avoiding the gravel path, Barbara led me to the stone wall that marked the edge of the policies and stopped at a 10-foot-wide gate. I could hear the river rushing past, urgent in the night.

"The water-gate," she said. "I'll leave you here."

"What do I do?" I asked.

"Row," Barbara said simply, vanishing back into the dark. I saw the flicker of her candle for a few seconds, and then it was gone. I was alone with the dark and the surge of the river.

Row? I opened the wooden gate and smiled in relief. Baird's skiff, *Nabob of Mysore*, was moored to a small jetty, with the oars shipped and the river lapping at the hull. Hitching up my skirt, I crouched down to untie her, stepped aboard and pushed off. I floated free for a few moments before sliding the oars into the water and pulling firmly. I closed my eyes; I had done it. Now all I had to do was row a short distance, head back to land and go home.

Kenny and my future waited.

CHAPTER 16

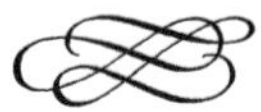

FIRTH OF TAY, MAY 1827

Or so I thought, but the gods of mischance were not yet finished playing with my hopes and dreams. The very instant I dipped my oars into the river, the wind rose. The Tay can be like that, one moment all silver and satin, smooth as cream and whispering sweet innocence, the next the wind roars in from the German Ocean, or across from the hills of Fife. That is what happened to me; as I guided *Nabob*'s bows into the Firth, the wind rose from the east. It caught me by surprise, nearly capsizing the skiff, so I had to fight frantically to regain my balance.

Thrusting the oars deep into the water, I rowed, with the current taking hold of *Nabob* and propelling me downstream faster than I had a mind to go. I could see the lights of Dundee to my left and those of Fife to my right, and knew that if I kept a course between them, I should be able to find my way, even at night. Unfortunately, dense clouds concealed both the moon and the stars so, although house lights illuminated the coasts, the water itself was dark; I could not see my immediate surroundings. With the wind coming from the east and the current strong from the west, the river chopped up rough, with waves crashing against the bow and hull of my skiff, and water surging inside. Within minutes my legs were soaked, and when I pulled hard, the bows dipped, shipping more water.

I looked around, preparing to steer for the northern shore, where the lights of Dundee winked invitingly. I could feel the wind on my back and knew it was pushing me inexorably westward, back towards Mysore House, so I pulled harder. If I had left the house only 10 minutes earlier, before the wind rose, I would be on dry land by now and safe. I pulled again, straining at the oars, and yelled as *Nabob of Mysore* crunched on to something solid. The impact threw me backwards into the bottom of the boat.

"What the deuce?" I borrowed some of Kenny's choice nautical words as I sprawled there, uncomprehending as the bows of *Nabob* thrust upwards and the river surged around the stern. Forcing myself upright, I peered into the dark.

I had run aground. The Firth of Tay is notorious for sandbanks, from the mouth all the way up nearly as far as Perth. Now, in my rush to reach Dundee, I had slid into one, possibly My Lady's Bank. When I heard the crunch of something on the sand, I knew that I was not alone. Something other than *Nabob* was on this sandbank.

My first thought was for Baird; had he followed me into the Tay? No; he could not for I had his boat. When my companion emitted a barking cough, I knew that it was a seal, for there are scores of them in and around the Tay. I wondered if seals were dangerous, decided it was best to keep clear and disembarked so I could push the skiff into the water. However, the second I began to push, I realised that *Nabob* was far heavier than I had thought; she was stuck tight in sucking sand, and I could not shift her an inch. The water was also receding as the tide ebbed; in the short space of time since I had driven ashore, the water had receded considerably. I stood miserably on that sandbank, knowing I was stuck there until the tide flowed again, or until somebody saw my predicament and came to rescue me.

It was then that I realised the full extent of my predicament; the wind had driven me back the full distance I had rowed, and now I was directly opposite Mysore House. Even as I stood there, I could see lights flickering in the upper windows as the servants woke for their day's labour.

I swore then; I freely confess that I used every word that I have ever heard so that any of the seamen on *Admiral Duncan* would have been impressed by my repertoire. What had I done to offend the gods of romance? I just wanted a simple life with a decent man, and here I was stranded on My Lady's Bank in the middle of the Tay, only a few hundred yards from a crazy woman who wished to marry me off to her equally demented son.

I nearly did myself a mischief trying to push that blasted boat into the water, with the same result as before. I lacked the strength to budge it one fraction, and the river water was still receding as the tide ebbed. The seals were making a devil of a racket now as more of them joined their companions, grunting and roaring fit to frighten the French. I had no idea they were such noisy creatures, or so large when one is close by them. As the lights of Dundee began to fade, I realised that dawn was fast approaching and soon half the world would see me standing forlornly on my sandbank. I would be the laughing stock of Dundee and Fife, my name and position would be in the newspapers and Kenny would be ashamed to be seen with such a foolish woman. I cursed most shockingly and again tried to push the boat free of the sandbank, without any success.

The lights blazed in Mysore House as the maids opened the shutters. I had seen the faint flicker of the maids' candles in the attic windows, but now the house was awake, and I did not have to ask why. Somebody had discovered my absence, and Baird and Mrs MacGillivray would be searching the house, interrogating the maids and checking every corner to find out where I was hiding. It was only a matter of time before somebody thought to check the water-gate or glance out the window and see me, standing on my sandbank like a castaway mermaid.

Could I swim for shore?

Perhaps. Thankfully the wind had dropped as suddenly as it had arisen. It had done its mischief and now retreated to wherever the wind lived when the gods did not send it to torment my hopes. With the light strengthening, I eyed the distance to the northern shore of the Tay – perhaps 300 yards. Now, that does not sound too much, and I am perfectly capable of swimming 300 yards in calm, mild water when I am suitably dressed, or rather suitably undressed. However, the Tay has a very powerful current and would undoubtedly drag me far from where I wished to land, while the presence of herds of seals was unsettling. I had no desire to feel them nibbling at my feet, or any other part of me.

Still undecided, I waited as the light strengthened and day dawned. I tried to shelter on the northern side of *Nabob* in the vain hope that the inhabitants of Mysore House would not see me.

I saw the figure at the topmost window of Mysore House and knew without doubt that it was Baird. I also knew he would see his boat and the figure beside it. Baird was intelligent enough to work out that I had stolen his boat. Now it was only a matter of time before he came for me, and the whole stupid game would start again.

It was nearly full daylight now, with a wan sun glinting off the wave tops. My sandbank was about 50 yards long and 10 wide and almost filled with barking seals, hard to miss for anybody looking over the firth. Then, when I saw the sun glint on something protruding from Baird's window I guessed he had fetched a telescope. I stood erect, determined not to cringe away from Baird MacGillivray. *Here I am, Baird,* I thought, *come and get me, gin ye daur* – if you dare.

By now vessels were sailing on the Tay, barges bringing stone down from Kingoodie Quarry, a cluster of fishing boats and a coaster or two sailing to Perth, but none would jeopardise their vessels by approaching a sandbank. Despite my earlier reservations, I resolved to swim to the shore before Baird located another boat and came to capture me. I had no choice.

Trying to avoid the seals, I walked across the sandbank to the spot nearest the northern shore, tucked my skirt up between my legs and measured the distance. Dundee was awakening, tantalisingly close. Taking a deep breath, I stepped as far as I could into the water and kicked for shore. I was a strong swimmer, if not a particularly fast one, but my long skirts soon became untucked and hampered me, slowing my progress to a painful crawl. The current was even stronger than I had expected, carrying me away from my intended landing point and down towards the docks. I spluttered as my strength began to fade and then I saw the horseman cantering to my left, from the direction of Mysore House.

Baird MacGillivray. He had mounted Zeus and was going to intercept me the second I landed in Dundee. I knew I could not swim faster than a horse could gallop and nor had I sufficient strength remaining to swim back to the sandbank. I was trapped, literally, between the deep blue of the Firth of Tay and the devil of Baird MacGillivray.

Baird rode Zeus until he was right opposite me, separated only by a few score yards of cold water. “Catriona!” He shouted out. “Catriona; it will be all right. Let’s talk about this.”

I had no intention of talking to Baird about anything. I trod water, with my strength failing and the weight of my clothes threatening to drag me down.

“I’ll come for you,” Baird called. I saw him urge Zeus into the river, walking until the horse was belly-deep, and then Baird slowly removed his top-coat and hat, then his long riding boots and weskit. For a moment I thought he would strip off his breeches too, but I was at least spared that unpleasantness as he slid into the water and began to swim towards me. I backed away, not knowing where to go and finding it harder to move every second.

I think that was one of the most unpleasant moments of my life, slowly sinking into the Tay with Baird swimming purposefully closer and the prospect of a lifetime of child-bearing servitude before me. Yet fate can sometimes be kind as well as cruel, and help can come from the most unexpected sources.

“There she is!” A young voice piped across the grey of the morning. “Over there.”

Low down in the water, with waves breaking over my head, I

could not see much except the prow of a boat coming from the east. I had lost sight of Baird, although I knew he was approaching. Baird was not a man to give up.

Something landed in the water close to me, a line of some sort, and that shrill voice sounded again. "Take hold, Miss!"

Eager for any way out, I grabbed for the line, missed and floundered, trying desperately to keep afloat but failing as the weight of my clothes finally overcame my strength. I felt myself slip under the water, heard the most infernal roaring and bubbling in my ears, and terrible burning pain in my throat and lungs.

So this was how drowning felt. This is how my father died, and so many thousands of seamen before him. I tried to kick myself back to the surface; I opened my mouth to yell and swallowed water that seemed to scorch my chest. I felt myself choking, and then something hard scraped across my hips and stuck into my person. Was this death? I felt no pain, only the sensation of being pulled upwards and then there was air and light and voices that seemed too loud to bear.

"Got her!" a man's voice roared. "Make space, Davie!"

The light was painful, and somebody seemed to be pummelling me from behind, pressing down heavily on my back. I vomited water, choked and groaned.

"That's my girl! Get rid of it!"

I knew that voice. I knew that voice very well indeed.

"More to come, Catty!"

The pressure came again, forcing the water from my lungs and leaving me as limp as any rag doll, face down in an undignified heap on the bottom of the boat that had rescued me.

"What the devil were you doing swimming at this time of the morning?" The voice was cheerful yet concerned.

Strong arms eased me into a sitting position and held me close. I struggled to escape, fearing that Baird had captured me.

"It's all right," Kenny reassured me. "You're safe now. I've got you."

I looked up, sodden, with my clothes a ragged mess around me and a new wound beginning to smart on the opposite side of my shotgun injury, I must have looked like the orphan from the storm, a bedraggled mess that no man would wish to know. And suddenly I knew that was not true. This man, Kenny Fairweather, did not care how I looked or what I wore or did not wear. I knew that by the expression in his eyes as he cradled me.

"Is she alive?" Young Davie from *Admiral Duncan* was grinning over Kenny's shoulder. "Halloa, Miss! It's me! Davie!"

I managed a weak smile that must have looked like the grimace of a condemned man. "Halloa, Davie. Where did you spring from?"

"I seen you standing on the sandbank," Davie said happily. "The cap'n sent us out to find you and I seen you, so I ran to tell him."

"Right," I said. "I'm glad you did." I closed my eyes as the misadventures of the past few days caught up with me. I only wanted to stay where I was, safe in Kenny's arms.

"So I telt the cap'n," I heard Davie's voice as through a fog, penetrating yet not unwelcome. "And the cap'n sez, 'Are you sure it was Miss Easson?' so I telt him that I was sure and he got the boat out and come up like the devil was prodding a pitchfork in his bum."

"Thank you, Davie," I said. "That was most graphic."

"Who was that man in the water?" Davie asked. "He was wanting no good. I kent that as soon as I seen him. I telt the cap'n that. I sed, 'See that man there, Cap'n,' I sed, he's a blackguard that yin, a black-hearted bugger if ever I seen one."

In my relief at being rescued, I had quite forgotten about Baird. I opened my eyes and sat up so abruptly that I set my head pounding and had Kenny reaching for me. "What's the matter, Catty?"

"Is he still there? Is that man still there?"

"We left him in the water," Kenny said. "That was Baird MacGillivray, wasn't it?"

"Yes," I said.

"Aye. I'll have words with Mr Mac later, once you are safe."

"No." I was surprised how decisive I was, given the

circumstances. "No, Kenny. Let things rest now. You've won, if you still want me, and I don't want any more silly competitions."

He smiled down at me with love shining from in his eyes. "I will always want you. I see I'll have to keep an eye on you in future. If I leave you alone, you get into all sorts of trouble."

"Where are we going?" I asked.

"Home. My house," Kenny said. "Lie still now. You've had a nasty fright there."

Now that I was recovering, I could not lie still any longer. Ignoring the thumping pain in my head, I sat up. Baird was only a forlorn figure in the distance, standing beside Zeus and watching as we powered downstream with the current.

"Why were you on a sandbank in the dawning, Miss?" Davie enquired.

I told them. Editing some parts out because of Davie's young ears, I told my story, with Kenny's face growing blacker by the sentence.

"I'll kill him," he said when I finished.

"No." I put my hand on his arm. "No. Let it end here, Kenny. We have more important things to discuss than Blair MacGillivray."

Looking at me, Kenny nodded. "He can wait," he agreed. "Your safety is more important than revenge."

"No, Kenny," I insisted. "It's not a matter of waiting. That episode is finished. Promise me."

Kenny held my gaze for a long moment before he nodded. "It's finished," he said.

"Thank you." I know what Kenny's decision must have cost him, and I knew I could trust his word.

Kenny gave quiet orders to Davie as we approached the docks. Davie proved very skilful in bringing us alongside, and I stepped ashore, sodden and shaky on my feet. Kenny was there to support me. "It's not far. Davie will look after the boat."

"Where will he go?" I looked at the young boy, left alone in the docks.

"He lives aboard *Admiral Duncan*," Kenny said. "It's the only home he's got."

I staggered a little as my various hurts began to ache, and did not object when Kenny lifted me as if I were a child. "You're too weak to walk," he told me, adding softly, "besides, I want to hold you."

Kenny's house was off Dock Street; a five-roomed place that he shared with his parents. "We're home!" he shouted as we approached the front door, which opened as if by magic.

"Here she is!" Kenny swept me inside the house. "Safe and sound, if a bit wet. Build a fire up and get the kettle on!"

Within seconds, smiling faces encircled me, with Mr and Mrs Fairweather stretching out hands to help, but more surprising was the third person in the room. My mother's smile could not have been wider.

"Mother!"

"Kenny and I have been talking about you." Mother's attempt to sound stern failed utterly. "He's been sending his crew to scour the town for you."

"He found me." I explained my movements since I had come ashore from Admiral Duncan. "I didn't know that Kenny had been so busy."

"He tried to get into Mysore House three times," Mother said.

"It's a fortress, that place." Kenny was busily building up the fire. "You'd better get some dry clothes on."

"All gentlemen will please leave the room," Mrs Fairweather ordered. "Out you go!" Mrs Fairweather was one of those plump, always-cheerful, happy women who keep the world turning when all others fail. I understood how Kenny could be so inarticulate with Mrs Fairweather in the house; she did not mind who spoke or who did not speak as long as they did as she ordered.

Once again, I found myself the centre of attraction as Mother and Mrs Fairweather towelled me dry, exchanging comments all the time.

"Look at the state of you!" Mother examined my shotgun wound and the small cut where Kenny had hooked me out of the water. "It's healing nicely, but you'll have a lovely dimple there!" She gave me her usual slap, which brought laughter from Mrs Fairweather, and some comments that I will not write down.

"I'll get these washed." Mrs Fairweather lifted my wet clothes.

"Not yet." I snatched them back. "I have something in there."

"Oh, secrets, secrets, always there are secrets," Mrs Fairweather said, smiling. "Come on, Catriona, get dressed before some inquisitive man peeks in."

Dressed in Mrs Fairweather's clothes, warmed by the fire and quite happy with life, I greeted Kenny with a smile. "Thank you for rescuing me," I said.

Kenny nodded. "Aye." He sat down on the far side of the room, smiling at me.

My old, monosyllabic Kenny was back. I did not care because I had seen the man beneath the silence.

"Kenny," I began, and stopped, aware of the expectant hush.

"Shall we leave you alone?" Mother showed surprising tact.

"Oh, no. I want to hear what Catriona has to say," Mrs Fairweather said. "Go on, Catriona, please pretend that we're not here."

I hid my smile. I wished to kiss Kenny quite passionately, and I certainly would not do that with so many people present. "Kenny, do you remember all that fuss about the brooch Barbara made for you?"

"Yes," Kenny's limited shoreside vocabulary did not make things any easier. He looked at me. "I lost that somewhere." He paused to think. "I wish I hadn't."

"I have it here," I handed the Luckenbooth brooch over.

I had never seen Kenny so surprised. "Good God. How did you come by this?"

I was about to say: "In your uncle's coffin." But I decided to leave that story for a later date. "I've had it for a while," I said instead. "I chased *Admiral Duncan* to give it to you."

Kenny looked confused. "Well, that's all past now. I've asked this before, but I'll ask again. Will you marry me?"

"Yes," I said. "Oh, yes, I'll marry you."

"Hold still," Kenny commanded and pinned the Luckenbooth brooch on to my breast. As the firelight reflected on the central ruby, I knew that everything would be all right. With that simple, traditional symbol, Kenny had confirmed his commitment, and no doubts were remaining. I would be Mrs Kenneth Fairweather, and that was both the end of it and the beginning.

CHAPTER 17

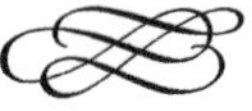

DUNDEE, JULY 1827

We married in St Mary's Church beside the Old Steeple, where my mother and I were regular members of the congregation. Mr Grieve did the needful, with his voice filling the great echoing spaces of the church and booming fit to frighten the French, although what the French have to do with my wedding I cannot tell you.

Naturally, with anything to do with the Fairweathers or the Eassons, the church was full to bursting, with weather-beaten seamen looking uncomfortable in their Sunday best, and prim wives keeping them under control.

I had spent time over my appearance, with a delicate blue dress that my mother and I had laboriously tailored to my rather buxom shape. As I stood at the altar with a church of supportive women and men behind me, I glanced at Kenny with his set mouth in his calm face, wondered how on earth I could get him to talk and shook my head. That did not matter as much as the man did. I would miss him when he was at sea, though. I would miss him terribly.

I was so busy thinking of the future that I nearly missed Mr Grieve's crucial words: "Repeat after me, 'I Catriona Sheila Easson.'"

"I Catriona Sheila Easson," I followed Mr Grieve's lead, aware of the expectant hush in the church behind me. "Take this man, Kenneth James Easson, to be my lawful wedded husband." I almost gabbled the words, in case somebody chose to interrupt the ceremony. I had a fear of Baird MacGillivray bursting in to spoil my day.

Mr Grieve gave a little nod of encouragement before turning to Kenny, who stood erect, staring in front of him. "Now you, Kenny." The minister's voice was soft.

"I, Kenneth James Fairweather, take this woman, Catriona Easson to be my wife, to have and to hold from this day forward, for better, for worse, for richer, for poorer, in sickness and in health, to love and to cherish, till death us do part, according to God's holy law." Kenny barked out the words as if challenging the Lord to try to stop him.

In the event, the Lord chose to allow the wedding to proceed.

"You may kiss the bride," Mr Grieve said, smiling with his eyes.

I stood still, knowing that Kenny would be too embarrassed to kiss me in front of so many people and expecting to have to take the initiative. I turned toward him, to be taken into his arms and most soundly kissed, so soundly that the congregation gave a subdued cheer and even Mr Grieve gave a small chuckle when Kenny eventually released me. I stood breathless and flushed as Kenny took hold of my hand and marched me past a sea of smiling faces towards the entrance of the church. I nearly missed the woman who sat right beside the door until she looked up and caught my eye.

Mother Faa gave me a lopsided smile and winked. "You survived your storm, I see," she said. "And Baird MacGillivray put Kenny into his true perspective."

"Yes, Mother Faa," I replied, and she laughed.

"You need have no doubts now," Mother Faa said. "You chose right." As she thrust her clay pipe into her mouth, a thin beam of sunlight caught her ring, and for a second I saw the pattern, with a circle of amber around a central ruby. I had no time to comment before Kenny hustled me outside.

I had not expected to see Mother Faa in the church, and I was even less prepared for the crowd that waited in the street outside. It seemed that most of the maritime population of Dundee had gathered to see a Fairweather married off to an Easson, both famous names among the seafarers.

"So that's you, then." Mother appeared at my side. "My last daughter happily married to a good man." I saw the tears in her eyes and wondered how she would cope without me. That thought eroded a fraction of my happiness.

Kenny squeezed my arm. "She'll be fine," he said.

"How did you know what I was thinking?"

"I'm your husband," he said. "I understand you. Did you see the way the minister looked over to your mother after the ceremony?"

I shook my head. "Somebody was kissing me at the time."

"So somebody was. Mister Grieve has set his cap at your mother, Catriona. She won't be alone for long."

For some reason, I glanced over my shoulder. Mother and the minister were standing side by side and, as I looked, I saw Mr Grieve's hand reach over and squeeze Mother's arm. I looked away hurriedly as Kenny guided me to our waiting carriage.

The wedding breakfast was in the Fairweathers' house where the funeral had been held. I looked at the Luckenbooth brooch at my breast as I walked in, and took my place at the table, still numb at the day's events. It all seemed unreal and I felt as if I was looking down at myself from above. I did not deserve such happiness.

Mrs Fairweather placed herself at my side, carrying on three different conversations simultaneously. She drank deeply from her glass of claret and smiled at me.

"Did you hear Kenneth's news?"

"No," I replied, and Mrs Fairweather continued, happy to have a captive audience.

"He's been made captain," she announced and I could feel the pride bursting through her. "After he brought *Admiral Duncan* home safely, the owners have given him command of *Admiral Nelson*."

"Oh, that is indeed good news," I said, remembering the larger vessel Kenny had shown me, although the full implications had not yet hit me.

"The owners are trying new routes," Mrs Fairweather said. "They want Kenny to take *Admiral Nelson* to Australia."

My elation collapsed. "Australia," I echoed. "That will be a terribly long voyage."

"Months and months," Mrs Fairweather said. "He might be away for a full year or more."

I felt sick at the thought of being newly married and then to have a year without Kenny. I saw him smiling at me. "I'm glad you got promoted," I said, trying to hide my disappointment, yet I had to add: "I'll miss you."

"No, you won't," Kenny said.

"I will." I hoped we were not heading for our first disagreement as a married couple.

"You won't miss one bit of me." Kenny was smiling. "I'll be the shipmaster, remember. That means I can take my wife with me."

"Oh," I said and then again, "oh," as the realisation dawned. I would be with Kenny on a long voyage to a new country, on board a ship, the place where he was at his best. I turned towards my mother to see her in deep conversation with Mr Grieve.

"What did I tell you?" Kenny said. "She'll be fine, and so shall we."

"Yes." I thought of long talks on deck as we sailed south. "We will." And I kissed my husband.

Dear reader,

We hope you enjoyed reading *Storm of Love*. Please take a moment to leave a review in Amazon, even if it's a short one. Your opinion is important to us.

Discover more books by Helen Susan Swift at https://www.nextchapter.pub/authors/helen-susan-swift

Want to know when one of our books is free or discounted for Kindle? Join the newsletter at http://eepurl.com/bqqB3H

Best regards,

Helen Susan Swift and the Next Chapter Team

HISTORICAL NOTE

Although this story is fiction and none of the characters existed, I based the historical background on fact. Dundee had a longstanding trade with the Baltic, and at that period was experiencing the industrial expansion which would see factories and mills dominate her streets. Many Scottish merchants sailed to India or other quarters of the Empire and returned with a fortune. Known as nabobs, they often bought large houses and lived in luxury.

In the 1820s, graverobbers were a plague to Scotland, digging up freshly-buried corpses to sell to anatomists, the doctors who taught anatomy to university students. Naturally unhappy that thieves were stealing their dead; communities built watch-towers and employed armed guards to repel them. The mass murders of Burke, MacDougall and Hare in Edinburgh finally forced the authorities to act. In 1832 the British government passed the Anatomy Act, which allowed anatomists legal access to more corpses and ended the illegal trade.

The River Tay was notorious for its fast current and dangerous sandbanks. Today it is pleasant to stand at Dundee's Riverside and watch the play of light over the water and sand, where seals still gather. For the old-time seamen, such obstacles were less welcome.

Helen Susan Swift

Dundee, Scotland, December 2019

You might also like:
When The Music Ends by Simone Beaudelaire

To read the first chapter for free, head to:
https://www.nextchapter.pub/books/when-the-music-ends-contemporary-romance

Lightning Source UK Ltd.
Milton Keynes UK
UKHW010751100920
369682UK00001B/120